Ohio Reading Circle
1979
6th

Tawny

TAWNY

By Chas Carner

Illustrations by Donald Carrick

MACMILLAN PUBLISHING CO., INC.
New York

Macmillan Publishing Co., Inc.
866 Third Avenue, New York, N.Y. 10022
Collier Macmillan Canada, Ltd.

Printed in the United States of America

10 9 8 7 6 5 4 3 2 1

LIBRARY OF CONGRESS CATALOGING IN PUBLICATION DATA

Carner, Chas.   Tawny.

SUMMARY: Twelve-year-old Trey Landry, adjusting
to the death of his twin brother, adopts
and cares for an injured doe.
[1. Death—Fiction.   2. Farm life—Fiction.
3. Deer—Fiction]   I. Carrick, Donald.   II. Title.
PZ7.C2177Taw   [Fic]   77–17411
ISBN 0–02–716700–3

*This book is dedicated to the
Ishee family, Edmund Landry and
my great-uncle Charles A. Link,
who taught me everything I know—
precious people who have
enriched my life.*

Part I

THE SMALL POND down the hill from the farmhouse had started freezing over during the long November nights. Every morning, right after their chores, the twin boys would race over the gray-frozen field to check the ice's thickness before the afternoon sun would begin to melt it away. "Watch. I'm going to throw this rock high into the air and see if it breaks through," Troy would say. "Don't," his brother would answer. "The rock will freeze into the ice and spoil the skating." So the two boys waited restlessly until even the sun was cold and the ice grew thicker and thicker.

But that was months ago. Now, the pond was covered with a heavy, black ice that groaned and settled into itself, shooting deep cracks across its surface and sounding like a big applewood log being split for the fire.

The boy glided over the glassy plane, silently studying the etchings his skate blades left behind. Sometimes, he would stop and study an oak leaf set deep into the clear ice. He remembered a photograph he had seen in school of an insect, millions of years old, trapped in amber-colored resin.

It had been a different kind of winter. Only a light dusting of snow had fallen so far, and the harsh, dry winds had blown it around like powder. The nights and mornings had been so cold that the snow collected in the frozen tire ruts felt like cornstarch under his work boots. The winds sifted the snow through the brown-brittle blades of grass in the fields, hissing as it pelted the dried leaves and windswept hay. It was a bad year for the animals, his father had said. "Grampa used to call these 'bald winters.' They freeze the ground and everything on it without a protective covering of snow."

The boy thought of these things as he circled the pond once more. Yes, it had been a very different year.

"Trey Landry, it's time for supper and I won't call you again." His mother's voice floated over the barren field from the kitchen door. He knew he still had a few minutes left. As the sun settled behind the pines on the hill he skated toward the edge of the ice where his boots waited stiffly. He sat on the ice close by and raised his skate-booted foot high. *Pik.* The back of his skate blade shattered the smooth surface and scattered ice chips around him. *Pik-pik.* The blade sunk deeper, the crater getting wider and wider. *Pik-pik-pik.* Harder and harder he chopped at the ice. Again and again he struck until, finally, the blade punched through and the bowl-shaped dent filled silently with water. He watched for a mo-

4

ment, then, crouching close, pushed his face toward the near-freezing water and drank, burning his lips and throat and stinging the tip of his nose.

"Didn't you hear me call you?" his mother asked as soon as the back door slammed shut behind him.

"Yes, ma'am," he answered, leaving his skates in the mud room and pulling his frozen mittens from his cold-stiffened hands. He squinted from the glaring light in the kitchen.

"I called you three times," his mother returned, not turning away from the stove where pots steamed and simmered. "Hang up your hat and coat and sit right down here at the table. You can wash your hands at the kitchen sink." The warm water hurt his hands, but he did not complain. He was more worried about not letting the big bar of soap slip onto the floor.

"Your father's late, too. He thinks the new Holstein's going to have that calf any minute. He'd like you to help him if it comes tonight."

The boy ate his supper quietly alone. An empty chair stared back at him from across the table. After he had finished eating, the boy carried his plate to the sink. Through the frosted window he could see his father approaching the back door.

"Looks like my guess was right. I've moved Ida into the calving pen," his father said, stamping his feet just inside the door.

"Do you want me to call Freddy Coombs and see if he can come over and help out?" his mother asked.

"Not right yet. Trey and I might be able to handle

5

it ourselves. What do you say, doctor? Are you ready to deliver another baby?" he asked his son.

"Yes, sir," Trey answered, drying his hands on the faded dishtowel and hurrying to pull on his hat and coat.

"Don't forget your mittens," his mother warned, pulling the boy's cap down over his ears. "I'll have some nice hot cocoa ready for you when you get back."

Trey and his father leaned into the wind as they made their way toward the barn.

"We'll probably have to help Ida this time, son. She's new at this sort of thing and she'll be pretty scared. I'll need you to keep her calm. Just talk to her, tell her what's happening. You know more about calving than she does."

Ida's bellowings could be heard through the night's wind. Trey ran ahead and struggled to drag open the heavy, sliding barn door.

It was warmer inside the unheated barn, mostly because there was no wind. Or, maybe it was just a different kind of coldness: heavier and quieter. The air always seemed thicker inside the barn, filled with the rich, sticky-sweet smells of hay dust, silage, grain and manure. Trey worried about the newborn calf's coming into such a frigid world. Winter births were always the hardest.

His father moved ahead, past the fifty other black and white cows rattling their stanchions and calmly chewing. They watched him walk by. Trey touched each of the animals' noses as he passed. One or two licked his hand with their sandpaper tongues. The calving room, or "nursery," was far in the back of the long barn. Ida stopped her bellowing when Trey and his father entered the musty, dimly lit room.

She stood rigidly in the center of the small, straw-covered floor, panting heavily and shaking nervously. Her breathing was deep and rhythmic. Trey knew what to do. He spread armloads of straw over the floor and gently ran his hands over the animal's swollen body. He could feel the calf struggling, deep inside, trying to set itself free. "Good Ida," he said in a voice much deeper and more soothing than he would ordinarily use. "Good mother."

He circled her once and pressed his face against hers. "You'll be all right, Ida," he said. "Just a little while longer."

His father pushed her hind flanks a little farther away from the wall. Ida moved obligingly.

Suddenly, her whole body shuddered and a gush of hot, steaming water poured onto the floor. "Here it comes," his father said. Trey scratched her under her neck and peered into her terrified eyes. "Okay, Ida. You're okay."

And slowly, ever so slowly, the calf began to emerge. First one hoof, then the other. Slowly. Ida strained and shivered and bellowed once. "Good momma," Trey soothed.

"We have to get her to lie down," his father said.

7

Trey tapped at the backs of the cow's front legs and pushed down on her head. "Down, girl," he said.

But Ida was confused and frightened. She moved suddenly to one side and slammed his father against the wall. "Hold on, Ida. Let's go back where we were before." His father pushed her back to the center of the room. She slipped once on the wet concrete. "You're doing just fine, Ida."

Her breathing became shorter and quicker. Great gulps of air moved in and out.

She went down! Without any warning, all four legs collapsed under her and within an instant she lay on the floor.

"Is she all right, Pa?" Trey asked.

"She's fine, son," his father answered. "Good girl, Ida," he said.

Nearly half an hour passed and still the calf had emerged no farther. They decided to help the calf and mother more. Trey handed the strands of baling twine to his father, who carefully wrapped them around the calf's front feet. And, slowly, his father began to pull. Slowly, steadily, he pulled harder and harder. Finally, the calf slid to the cold floor.

"It's a girl!" Trey heard his father say, happily. "A beautiful baby girl!"

The cow and calf lay peacefully for a moment. They must be exhausted, the boy thought. Ida rose slowly on unsteady legs.

Trey and his father stood close together and

watched the new mother turn and recognize the baby as her own. "She knows what to do now," his father said. And Ida began gently licking the shivering, steaming wet calf that huddled close to the ground at her feet.

"Your mother named the last calf. It's your turn this time. Do you have a name for her?" his father asked.

"Adi," Trey replied, staring at the trembling, pink-nosed calf that he had just helped to deliver into the world. How tiny she looked, he thought. And perfect. He felt proud of himself and of his father.

"We should leave them alone until morning. Are you about ready to have that hot chocolate?"

"Yes, sir," Trey replied, suddenly feeling very tired.

Chick-a-dee-dee-dee. . . . Chick-a-dee-dee-dee-dee. . . The tiny, comic gray-and-black bird hopped from one twig to another on the winter-bare lilac bush outside his window. Its buzzing voice called to Trey to wake up. From his bottom bunk, he could tell this was a gloomy Sunday. The steel-blue sky promised a flat day: the kind with no shadows and no wind.

Chick-a-dee-dee-dee-dee, called the little bird, merrily rustling among the dried clusters of once-violet flowers, and looking more like a wind-up toy with its every move.

He carefully slid out from under the covers and pulled the blankets and bedspread taut. The bed was made, his first chore of the day over. He quickly checked the top bunk. It looked exactly as it had the morning before, and every morning before that since last November when he had lost his brother. He thought of how he and Troy used to argue over who was to sleep in the coveted top bunk. It always seemed that Trey lost out. But it did not seem to matter much any more. He had decided long ago to leave his brother's bed alone, waiting, almost as if Troy were expected to return.

Chick-a-dee-dee-dee-dee, said the bird, hanging upside-down from a leafless branch and peering through the glass at the boy inside.

"If you stay very still and hold your arm out, they'll come and eat out of your hand," Troy said once. And he stood for hours, motionless, until one of the brave little birds lit upon his hand and accepted his breadcrumb offerings.

Troy always seemed to have a way with wild animals that Trey could never hope to equal. One fall, two years ago, a skunk would arrive every night at the Landrys' back door to rummage for food. Dutifully, Troy used to collect the table scraps to feed the animal. Aroma, she was called, and she would snarl and hiss and back away into the darkness as soon as Troy opened the back door. But Troy was patient, and eventually the skunk grew accustomed to his voice and would approach the boy boldly, hopping and bouncing in the puddles of light from the lamp overhead. "Dancing for her dinner," Trey used to say, safely inside the kitchen.

And then, one night, Aroma arrived as usual, but did not come near. She hid in the shadows and rustled among the leaves. Calmly, Troy walked toward the frightened animal, crouching low and speaking softly. Somehow, Aroma had managed to get her head stuck inside an empty jar and, in a frantic attempt to free herself, had shattered the suffocating enclosure. A jagged collar of glass remained that cut deeply into the animal's neck.

"Don't go near her, she'll bite you. She'll *spray* you," Trey warned from inside. But Troy continued drawing nearer and nearer. He touched the skunk lightly. It did not run away. And, slowly, gently, he removed the hideous ring of glass from around the animal's neck.

"Here. A souvenir," Troy said to his brother as he entered the kitchen. Trey kept the deadly collar in an old cigar box on his desk.

The skunk did not return after that night until the following spring when, one evening, Aroma arrived with three tiny babies that played together like kittens nearby while their mother ate her supper. But even they stopped coming after Troy died.

Only the jagged collar remained.

—2—

"WHAT'S GOING ON?" Trey asked the feet dangling in front of him from the bunk above.

"Shhh," his brother answered, "you'll wake Ma and Pa."

"Where are you going?" Trey persisted, sleepy-eyed and a little cranky from being so suddenly awakened.

"You'll see. Come on."

"*Where?*"

Troy dropped to the floor beside the bed. Trey was surprised to see that his brother was completely dressed. Troy pulled down his pillow and peeled away its white cotton cover.

"You're going to swipe apples again, aren't you?"

"Uh-huh. Old Mr. Atwood won't miss them. He's got a whole orchard full," Troy returned.

"No."

"No, what?"

"No, I'm not going."

"Okay," said Troy with a shrug. He opened the bedroom door to see if the hallway was clear. A stripe of white light broadened across the ceiling and opposite wall.

"Wait, Troy, don't go."

"I'll be back in a little while." He slipped out of the room and closed the door.

Trey scrambled to dress before his brother disappeared into the night. He pulled a sweater over his pajama top and hopped one foot at a time as he tugged at his jeans. Grabbing a pair of socks, he hurried toward the back door where he slipped into his work boots. Troy was already gone. Trey stuffed a flashlight into his coat pocket and ran out into the late October night.

The air was crisp and still, the sky was clear and India-ink blue and the full moon shone brightly, casting a silver light upon the ground.

"I thought you weren't coming," said Troy as soon as his brother had caught up.

"I changed my mind," Trey answered, panting from his run through the field.

"Aren't you afraid of what Ma will say if she finds out?"

"Aren't you?"

The boys walked quietly together over the pasture. Prickly juniper bushes scratched against their stiff-denimed legs. Trey tripped once on a branch from the ground-hugging evergreens. He felt clumsy and fool-

13

ish, although his brother said nothing, only waited for Trey to catch up again.

"We'll bring the apples to school tomorrow and you, Joel and I can give them out at recess."

"Johnny Atwood won't like that," Trey warned. Johnny, the orchardman's son, was one year older than the twins and he liked to sell his apples for a nickel apiece to his eighth-grade classmates.

"I know," Troy said with a smile. "But he won't do anything. Not with Joel around." Joel Ducharme, Troy's best friend at school, was the tallest boy in class and was the star center on the junior high basketball team.

They climbed over the stone wall and moved through the young pine grove that separated the farm from the neighboring orchard. Slipping expertly under the barbed-wire fence, the brothers ran through the gnarled apple trees, careful not to slip on the sweetly rotting fruit underfoot.

"Where did you go?" Trey called, suddenly confused and looking in every direction for his brother.

"Up here," Troy answered. He sat on an upper limb, carefully selecting the heavy, ripe McIntosh apples one at a time. The pillowcase fluttered to the ground.

"Here. Start packing." And Trey accepted each apple from his brother, gently placing them in the sack so as not to bruise them. They picked their share in no time at all. But Troy made no move to climb down.

"Come up here," Troy whispered. Trey climbed

14

higher and higher, leaving the harvest-laden sack below.

"What is it?"

"Look," said Troy as he pointed eastward.

A solitary buck stood elegantly amid the apple trees a few hundred feet downwind. Cautiously but confidently he moved; his antlers looked metallic in the moonlight. Behind him, farther down the rolling hill, the lights of the Atwood house shone brightly, but he did not seem to care. With the measured grace of a ballet dancer, he circled the area.

"That's the one John Steck will be after come hunting season, I bet," Troy whispered.

Trey did not have time to feel sad. "Look!" he said, pointing toward the pines nearby. A doe floated easily over the barbed-wire fence. She touched to ground lightly and trotted warily to the buck's side. A second and third doe appeared and, finally, a younger buck moved boldly into the open field. They stood together, motionless, the younger male keeping a safe distance from the older. And then, as if on signal, they spread out over the area to browse leisurely among the apple trees.

The boys studied the deer silently for a long time, watching them as they stretched their slender necks to nibble the low-hanging leaves and branches and eat from the dropped apples at their feet.

"They're so brave. Look how close they come," Trey said.

"This is their home," Troy answered matter-of-factly. He shinnied down the tree. "Come on, let's get back," he said, slinging the lumpy pillowcase over his shoulder.

Trey watched for a minute longer as the big buck flicked his white tail once and the herd loped silently away into the protective darkness, their white tails held high.

"Your father thinks we'll be shoveling snow before the day is out," his mother said with a good-morning kiss. "He says there's a big storm coming down from Canada. He's out covering some of the equipment right now."

The boy sat down to a breakfast of scrambled eggs, sausages and buttered toast. He poured himself a glass of milk from the glass pitcher on the table. This was real milk, he thought: heavy, aromatic and rich with cream and butter fat. "Fresh from the 'factory,'" his father would say. The milk at home was worlds apart from the watery-weak, homogenized stuff he was forced to drink in school.

He was glad to hear the news of the expected blizzard. At last the ground would be protected by a thick blanket of snow which would eventually melt and soak the fields to start the growing season in April. But the skating will be ruined, he thought. No matter. He would take a snow shovel and cut a maze on the ice to follow.

"I saw Adi yesterday," his mother continued cheerfully. "She's a pretty one, isn't she? And she's growing so fast. She'll be bigger than you are by spring."

The calf had grown quickly. No longer a fragile infant, she seemed to develop faster and stronger every day. And she had learned to recognize Trey and to moo happily whenever he approached with the rubber-nippled weaning bucket. Already she had become more independent and could be separated from her mother without putting up a fuss. "She's a prize-winner," his father had said.

"I'm going out to see if there's anything I can do to help your father with the equipment. We'll have to put the blade on the tractor before the snow starts. Be sure to finish your milk." His mother kissed him again before she left the kitchen.

"This is the easy listening sound of WTSM, bringing you music and news on a snowy February afternoon. . . ." The dusty, cobwebbed radio chassis in the barn played day and night. The music soothed the cows, his father had told him. Trey stared at the glowing vacuum tubes and the torn paper speaker gaping toward him. The radio was older than he was, he thought. ". . . Yes, sir, the tri-town area is going to be moving a little slowly for the next couple of days until the roads are cleared. In fact, reports from all over New England indicate that this first storm of 1958 is the worst blizzard in thirteen years. I bet the ski areas are happy today. . . ."

Trey knew the storm would last through the night.

Outside, the sky was filled with great feathery snow-flakes that fell fast and thick upon the frozen ground. The wind rattled the heavy barn doors and pushed great drifts against the north side of the building. Snow sifted inside through the cracks by the floor. There would be no school tomorrow.

". . . We'll have a full list of official cancellations in just a few minutes," the radio announcer continued. But Trey did not wait to hear the news. He had work to do.

Adi stretched her neck through the slats of the nursery and sucked greedily on the white nipple at the bottom of the weaning bucket. Trey held the galvanized pail by its wire handle with both hands and watched the level of the milk and vitamin solution drop lower and lower.

"Sorry I'm late, Adi," Trey said. "But I had to help Pa cover over some of the machinery before I could feed you."

Adi paid little attention to his words.

". . . The road commissioners and school boards have just announced that there will be no classes held at the public schools of Nashua, Hudson, Pelham and Litchfield tomorrow. . . ."

Trey never could understand his brother's delight at being excused from classes for a day or two. They only had to be made up at the end of the school year in June. He would much rather go to school now, even in bad weather, and not have to waste all those sunny days later on.

". . . I repeat, there will be no classes in Nashua, Hudson, Pelham and Litchfield tomorrow. . . ."

The radio did nothing to calm the flock of chickens housed in the little coop attached to the north side of the barn. The gusty, cold wind threw the squawking birds into a flurry of commotion. Even before Trey opened the wire mesh door, the chickens scurried, flapped and fluttered around their coop. He noticed that they had begun to shred the thick, protective insulation on the walls and that two of the heat lamps hung from the ceiling swung back and forth whenever a nervous bird collided with them in its attempt to fly up to the rafters. "These are Barred Plymouth Rock pullets," his father had informed him. "They are extremely high-strung and must be handled very carefully. Always be sure to move very slowly and to talk to them whenever you enter the coop. Otherwise, they may panic and injure themselves." But no matter how slowly Trey moved that day, the two dozen black-and-white hens exploded into frantic commotion. He hated collecting eggs, especially on days like this.

Gently, he removed the ivory-colored eggs from the laying boxes and placed each one into his basket. He collected eleven eggs. A bad day for laying, he thought. And before he left he scattered a little more cornmeal and laying mash around the floor, hoping the extra food would help to calm them. It did not and he was not surprised.

"Chickens are dumber than rocks," Troy had said once. Trey agreed.

By the end of the next evening's milking, the snow had stopped and the weather had warmed just enough that a cold, misting rain soaked their coats as Trey and his father walked back to the house.

"Going to be a pretty morning tomorrow," his father said.

Trey felt his jeans stiffen as the water froze on his legs. It was a good thing his mother had ordered his new long johns at Christmas, he thought. His old ones were worn through at their baggy knees.

He knew the sound instinctively. As he lay on his bunk, Trey heard the haunting, echoing howls and yelps a mile away. A pack of dogs was forming.

The boy peered out his window, through the ice-sheeted glass, through the now-crystalline lilac branches that clicked together in the gentle wind. The entire countryside was covered with ice. It was beautiful, he thought, as he stared, wide-eyed, at the morning light playing off the millions of prisms coating the bare-leafed maple tree in the yard. Diamonds!

He hurried into the kitchen where his father quietly cleaned and oiled his lever-action Winchester rifle. He could see a pair of his father's snowshoes stuck upright into the snowdrift outside the kitchen window.

"Freddy Coombs just called," his father said. "He says there's a pack of dogs running deer this way. I'm going to meet him at the crossroads. I'd like you to stay here with your mother and help her in the barn." He threw home the lever on his rifle and squeezed the trigger, easing the hammer back with his thumb. Trey watched his father walk out the back door.

The boy stood for a moment at the kitchen window as his father strapped the webbed snowshoes to his boots. He stood up slowly and smiled at his son inside the warm house. Then, mechanically, he slid cartridge after cartridge into the rifle's magazine. Trey waved good-by.

With long, gliding steps, his father set out across the thick-crusted snow. He moved effortlessly down the long, sloping hill, crossed the snow-covered pond and disappeared into a fairyland of sparkling trees.

"Poachers!" Troy hissed through clenched teeth. He stared out the back window into the November night. The boys could hear the faint hoots and hollers of the dozen or so hunters who beat their way through the forest on the other side of the pond, driving the terrified animals toward the two or three men who waited for the deer to stumble into range. "Like shooting fish in a barrel," one boisterous hunter had bragged once. Trey thought the man disgusting.

"But our land is posted," Trey protested. He saw an occasional flicker of a flashlight through the trees.

"What do they care? It isn't even hunting season yet!" Troy stormed out of the room.

"What are you going to do?"

"I'm going to kick them off our farm, that's what I'm going to do," Troy shot back.

"Don't! We can call Pa. Or call the game warden," Trey tried to reason with his brother.

"By the time Ma and Pa get back here from their stupid town meeting, those hunters will have killed every deer on the hill. I'm going out there and stop them."

"You can't do that! They won't listen to you. Don't go, Troy, it's dangerous." Trey tried to grab the jacket from his brother's hands.

"I'll yell plenty loud and they'll listen to me. Let go of my coat!"

"No! You can't go out there." Troy burst out the kitchen door, leaving his jacket in his brother's hands.

"Troy, come back here!" he screamed, but Troy ran off into the night. "Please don't go," Trey pleaded.

Troy could be mistaken for a deer in the darkness. He could be injured, Trey said out loud to himself. He had to find help. Someone who could stop Troy before it was too late. Freddy Coombs, he thought. He lived just over the hill.

Trey ran to the phone and dialed frantically.

"Come on," he said. "Please, somebody, answer the —Mr. Coombs? This is Trey Landry. I need your help. My folks are in town for the meeting and there are poachers on the land and Troy just went out to stop them. Could you please—"

"I'll be right there." Freddy slammed down the receiver before Trey could answer. It would take at least ten minutes for him to drive his pickup to the Landry farm. Trey looked at the clock on the wall. It was eleven minutes to nine.

Trey ran out to meet the truck as it pulled into the driveway. Freddy leaned out the window. "Get in," he said urgently. Trey scrambled to the passenger side.

One—two shots echoed over the hills! "Oh, my God!" gasped the old farmer as he slammed the accelerator to the floor and fishtailed across the lawn. Trey pointed the way, too terrified even to speak. They bounced wildly over the field, around the pond and up the rise toward the stand of tall pines. With broad, sweeping turns Freddy scanned the night with his headlights. Trey, thrown side-to-side in the cab, searched desperately through the trees at the forest's edge for a sign of his brother.

The truck skidded to a stop and Freddy Coombs threw open the door and removed his shotgun from its rack behind him in one motion. "You stay here, son, and keep the engine running." He walked into the black night, stopping only once to crack his gun over his arm and to slide two shells into the chambers. With a sudden jerk, the gun snapped shut. Trey saw him flick on his searchlamp as soon as he was out of the headlights' range. He disappeared into the darkness.

Trey wanted to go along, but he knew it was better to stay there with the truck in case Troy should come out on his own. He searched the clearing for his brother. He's all right, Trey told himself. Troy is all right.

Silence. The air was calm and the forest became very still. The only sound he heard was the rhythmic *tick-tick-tick* of the idling motor. Should he call out? he wondered.

A low, anguished moan reached the boy from the woods. "No! Please, dear God, no!" Trey sobbed. He waited for Freddy's and Troy's return.

The old farmer appeared among the silent pines. He carried Troy's body in his arms and staggered under the weight. Frozen in his seat, Trey watched their approach. Freddy had carefully wrapped the boy in his own jacket. Troy's arm dangled lifelessly, swaying with the farmer's heavy steps.

"He's dead, Trey. He's dead."

3

"TREY, I NEED YOU," his father called through a narrow part in the sliding doors. The boy set down the grain scoop he held and ran to the front of the barn.

"Get these things off my feet. I can't put her down just yet." The man cradled in his arms a shivering and bleeding yearling doe, wrapped in his red wool coat. Trey knelt and quickly unstrapped the snowshoes from his father's boots.

"Now, move Adi out of the nursery and put down some new straw bedding. Your mother's calling the vet. She's coming with a clean sheet and some warm water, but I forgot to tell her to bring a blanket. You'll have to run to the house and fetch it."

The boy did not wait to study the wounded doe. He led the calf to its mother's side and swiftly raked out the floor of the pen before spreading down a thick covering of new hay. His father waited, still holding the trembling animal. His face was red from the cold trek home through the fields. "Quickly now," he said, and Trey bolted out the door to the house.

He ran easily atop the deep snow's icy crust. Just like a dog, he thought. But a deer, with its slender hooves, punches through the crust as it runs which makes it easy prey for a pack of long-winded dogs.

He met his mother in the kitchen. She was holding a sheet for bandages as she stood by the sink, filling a bucket with water.

"Doc Sherburne's on his way," she said. "The poor thing," she added, almost to herself. She hefted the pail and walked to the back door, being careful not to slosh any water onto the floor.

"I'll meet you out there," she said, and left the house.

Trey clutched the blanket close to his chest as he ran back to the barn. His left foot broke the crust's surface and he sank, knee-deep, into the frozen powder beneath. The blanket broke his fall against the ice, but he gashed his chin. A tiny circle of blood was left behind.

"You're bleeding," his mother said as he entered the calving pen.

"I fell," he explained, not caring about his own condition. He stared, nearly hypnotized, at the doe quivering on her side in the straw.

"She's in shock. Keeping her warm right now is as important as treating her wounds." His father carefully covered the animal with the blanket and tucked it close around her. He left her hind legs exposed.

The ravenous dogs had shredded the helpless

doe's hindquarters. Deep gouges oozed burgundy-colored blood. Flaps of skin hung limply from her wounds. The exposed muscle twitched erratically.

"We got three of them. Two others ran off with their tails between their legs," said his father. "Shot two beagles and a German shepherd. What a waste. I wish those damned city folks would keep their pets to home."

It was common knowledge that every fall, when the foliage was at its peak, people from the city would drive through the countryside, sightseeing. Occasionally, an owner would abandon his dog, thinking it kinder to let the confused animal live in the wild than in the city or be destroyed by the Humane Society. They never stayed around to see their once-beloved pet starve to death or be shot for running deer.

The young doe lay at the boy's feet, passive and exhausted. Shallow breaths stirred her body sporadically. Trey saw the terror in her eyes, but knew she was too weak to try to escape.

"Make some bandages for me," his father said, handing the boy the sheet and his hunting knife. Trey began tearing the material into long strips.

Mrs. Landry knelt beside the animal; gently, she began to bathe the ragged wounds with warm water. "The doctor will be here soon, pretty girl. You'll be all right," she said soothingly. She washed away the blood from the doe's soft winter coat.

"Freddy Coombs said he'd stop by later to see how

27

she is doing," said Trey's father. "I hope she lasts that long."

Trey gazed at the helpless doe, praying that she might live.

The doctor arrived within forty-five minutes, carrying a heavy bag and bundled in thick clothes. His pant legs and boots were encrusted with snow.

"It's murder getting up your hill, Joe," he said. "The road's drifted shut and I had to leave the car and walk the last quarter mile." He peeled off his black leather gloves and extended his hand.

"Thanks for coming so quickly, Doc," returned Mr. Landry, grasping the doctor's hand in his.

"God help her," said the vet upon entering the nursery. "She looks pretty bad, Joe. Maybe the best thing we can do for her is put her out of her misery right now."

*

"No-o-o-o-o!" screamed his mother from the living room. Trey lay on his bed in the next room, exhausted from weeping for over half an hour. His mother's sobbing filled the house.

"How?" he heard his father ask, dazed. "Why?"

"It was an accident," said the police chief, Ralph Boutwell. He had been patrolling in his car when he received the radio call and had arrived only minutes before. Freddy Coombs and the policeman began the long, painful process of explaining what had happened while Trey's parents were away. Trey tried not to hear their words.

"I tried to have Stella reach you at the town hall, but you'd already left. I got here as soon as I could," Trey heard the police chief say at last.

"Where's Trey?" he heard his mother ask.

"In his bedroom," said Freddy Coombs. "He said he wanted to be alone."

Trey did not notice his mother enter the room. She knelt on the floor beside the bed and pressed her face into her son's chest. He held her for over an hour. He had cried himself out. It was her turn now.

"I can't promise anything, but if you leave me alone with her for a little while I'll see what I can do," said Doc Sherburne after the family had begged him for a chance to let the deer live. He pulled away his heavy gray coat and rolled up the sleeves of his flannel shirt.

They left together, worried but relieved that the doctor had decided to try to save the animal's life.

"I want to stay here," Trey told his parents.

"Just stay out of the way, son," his father replied.

"I will."

The boy climbed the ladder into the hayloft and nestled close to the opened trap door. He could see the doctor below working carefully, trying to piece back together the doe's injured legs. It would be a long and tiring job for both the doctor and his patient.

It was quiet in the loft. By summer, the swallows and pigeons would return to their nests in the rafters and they would fill the shadowed space overhead with their chirps and coos. But they were all gone now, abandoning their straw homes for some warmer, more comfortable clime. And, come spring, the elusive barn cats would burrow deep between the bales of hay and secretly give birth to their litters of kittens. It was Trey's job, now, to hunt them out alone.

"If we had another dog like Jippy, he'd keep those barn cats so busy running they wouldn't have time to have kittens," Troy said. The boys wedged themselves between the bales and tried to reach the nest of week-old kittens. They could hear their continuous, muffled mews.

"But Pa said we wouldn't get another dog ever again. Not after what Jippy did to the chickens," Trey returned.

"Well, we've got to do something or we're going to be crawling with cats by September."

"Old lady Johnson wants these ones," Trey said.

"Yeah, but what about the next litter? And the one after that? Mrs. Johnson isn't going to want all of them, you know. And Pa won't drown them like Amelia Jeskowitz does."

They finally reached the three tiny kittens and placed them in a straw-filled box where they would live for the next four or five weeks until they were old enough to be separated from their mother. The mother cat crouched low in the corner and hissed at the boys.

"Maybe we should try to have the mother cats fixed by Doc Sherburne, then," Trey suggested.

"We've got to catch them first."

So the boys worked patiently, trying to tame the nearly wild cats. Gradually, Troy and Trey won the trust of two of the three female cats, Alice and Wendy. And, on the day old Mrs. Johnson chugged away in her 1937 Chevrolet with the three kittens, the two mother cats were scooped up and placed into a wooden chicken cage and delivered to Doc Sherburne's office in town where the operations were performed. Only Katie, the third mother cat, escaped that fate. And Alice and Wendy never again came close to the boys.

For two hours Trey lay in the hayloft. He watched the doctor's every move: the administering of sedatives and anesthetics, the cleansing of the wounds with complicated medications, the painfully slow process of suturing together the animal's tattered legs and the gentle bandaging at the end. Trey thought that someday he would like to become a veterinarian.

"You can come down now, Trey," Doc Sherburne called. He filled a final hypodermic needle with antibiotics to ward off infection.

"You and your folks took pretty good care of her before I arrived. Nice job. She's young and strong and has a chance. A *slim* one, but a chance just the same. Now, the next few days are going to be the most important. It is essential that she begin eating and drinking plenty of water right away."

Trey knew that was not going to be easy. Wild animals—even healthy ones—usually give up all hope of living once they are in captivity. They simply stop eating and slowly starve themselves to death.

"Keep her calm, rested and fed and we might just be lucky enough to keep her alive. That's about all I can do for the time being. I'll leave these medications with Joe when I report in at the house. I'll stop by day after tomorrow and change those bandages. See you then." He pulled on his coat and left the barn.

Trey stood over the sedated animal, his hands crammed deep into his pockets. The look of vivid fear had left her eyes, but her breathing was still shallow and unsteady. It would be a cold night, he thought. Once the tranquilizer wore off she would be confused and frightened. He would stay beside her that night and try to keep her calm and warm.

He told his father of his intentions while they milked the cows that evening before supper.

"We figured you'd want to," Mr. Landry responded. "So your mother's making your supper right now. She'll bring it out here in a little while. I'll make sure she brings you a blanket, too." Trey was glad his parents understood.

Ordinarily, milking time was a quiet, peaceful point in the day. The mellow music from the radio and the rhythmic *chuck-chuck-chuck* of the shiny, quadropus milking machines soothed people and beasts alike. But, this night, everyone and every thing seemed aware of the suffering animal in the nursery nearby.

Periodically, Trey peeked into the calving pen to check on the doe. No matter how quietly he opened the gate, the deer startled and tried to stand. She still had not touched her food and water. Trey worried that maybe she already had given up hope.

Adi nuzzled her mother, seemingly pleased at having been set free of the pen. Ida mooed softly as Trey walked past. She was impatient for her ration of ensilage and grain. She pressed her big nose into the cast-iron watering bowl attached to her stanchion and opened its spring-loaded valve. The water hissed and bubbled and Ida drank her fill. She bellowed once more.

"Shhh. You'll frighten the doe," Trey said sternly. But he knew that was not true. The deer and the cattle in the area were well acquainted and, in the summer, it was not uncommon to see deer moving among the herds of grazing cows.

"How's she doing?" asked Freddy Coombs. Neither Trey nor his father had seen the man enter the barn.

"Not too well," Trey answered. "She keeps thrashing around and she won't even drink water."

"Doc Sherburne gives her about a one-in-ten chance," Mr. Landry added.

"Well, Joe, if there's anybody in this town that can pull her through, it's you and the boy."

"I'm going to stay with her tonight," Trey said.

"Good. Keep her warm and quiet. Mind if I take a look?" He moved toward the calving pen and, before

Trey could warn him about frightening the doe, he opened the gate. "She looks pretty calm now. Didn't budge at all. Doc Sherburne did a good job of patching her back up, too. I bet she's got more like a forty-sixty chance of making it." Trey's hopes rose at his words.

"Now, Fred, don't go getting the boy all excited," his father said. "Nobody's going to know anything until it happens."

With the milking and feeding completed, Trey said good night to his father and Mr. Coombs. They walked back to the house, he walked back to the nursery with his blanket and paper-sacked supper.

At first, he sat cross-legged in the corner of the pen, giving the doe plenty of room and a chance to settle into his presence. She did not stir, but watched him cautiously. Trey nibbled quietly at his sandwich, avoiding the deer's eyes with his own and trying not to move too quickly.

"Tawny," he said softly at last. The doe perked up her ears and Trey inched a little closer.

"I'll call you Tawny, how about that?" She dropped her ears and looked away. The boy figured the response better than nothing.

"It's a pretty name, don't you think?" He moved a little closer.

A barn cat shinnied up a rough-hewn beam close by and curled itself into a tight ball on the rafter overhead. She watched the scene below. Tawny did not seem to mind the intruder.

"I think it's a pretty name," the boy continued. "My name is Trey. I'll take good care of you and you're going to get better and better every day. You're safe here. All you have to do is eat your food and drink lots of water like a good girl." Trey slid the water pail closer. She jerked away from the sudden noise. He could reach out and touch her now if he tried, but he decided to wait.

Trey and his mother entered the living room. His mother held tightly onto his hand. His father sat on the sofa and looked into the smoldering fire. The police chief stood in the middle of the room, trying to fill the space with his steady compassion. He approached them and held Trey's mother's hands in his.

"I'm sorry, Barbara," he said. His face was gaunt and ashen. He spoke in a whisper.

"I know, Ralph. I know." Her words dropped heavily to the floor. "We thank you for coming as soon as you could. For being here."

Freddy Coombs came in from the kitchen, carrying a fresh pot of coffee. He refilled Mr. Landry's cup.

Through the window, Trey saw an ambulance parked in the driveway. Two men waited outside for the signal to enter the house. They shivered from the night's cold and passed a cigarette between them.

The clock on the mantel told him it was almost midnight. Trey sat on the floor beside his father and rested his head against his father's leg. He felt a gentle hand stroking his hair.

35

It's my fault, Trey thought. I should have stopped him. If I had stopped him, Troy would be alive. It's all my fault.

Finally, the men from the ambulance entered the front door. They spoke briefly and quietly to the police chief. And then Troy's body, wrapped in a white blanket, was placed on a stretcher and carried from the sewing room beside the kitchen to the vehicle. Freddy and Mr. Boutwell closed the doors in back.

They stood in the doorway as the ambulance pulled away slowly into the night. Trey waved good-by to his brother.

"I'll call you in the morning, Joe," the police chief offered. "Let me know if there's anything I can do."

"Thanks, Ralph. Freddy." His father shook the men's hands. Mr. Coombs embraced the boy's mother, then held Trey by the shoulders at arms' length and looked into his face. He spoke no words, but Trey understood.

Before the police car rolled out of the driveway, Trey heard the garbled radio reports on the police's attempts at apprehending the men who had killed his brother. Trey was sure they would never be caught.

Freddy Coombs' pickup truck followed the police car down the road.

The house felt empty and black. No one spoke. There was nothing to say. Not yet.

The family spent the rest of the night together in the living room. His mother huddled on the couch and struggled through a restless sleep. She rested her head on her husband's lap and he cradled her in his arms. It was the first time Trey had ever seen tears in his father's eyes.

"We'll be all right, Pa," Trey comforted.

"I know, son," his father whispered. His lower lip quivered as he spoke. He sighed and looked at his son.

"I miss him," Trey said.

"So do I. This never would have happened if I had stayed home tonight."

"It's not your fault, Pa," Trey said. He realized then that each of them wrestled with his own guilt. "It just happened is all."

But even Trey's own words could not comfort him.

His legs ached from sitting in one place for so long, but Trey did not dare to stretch out. He drew closer to the doe whenever he thought the time was right. He moved slowly and delicately so as not to frighten her any more. He pulled his blanket close around his head and shoulders. Tawny shivered and remained awake.

She had not touched the water.

"You have to drink, Tawny," Trey urged. "You haven't had anything all day. Please don't give up on me, girl."

She watched him closely as he dipped his hand into the frigid water, cupped it for a minute, then poured it back into the pail. A drop splashed onto her mouth and the tip of her tongue caught it before it reached the floor. She drank!

Trey moved beside her and touched her for the first time. Lightly, with the tips of his fingers.

"Water, Tawny," he said. And he cupped a little more of the liquid in his hand and brought it near her mouth. "Here."

She licked his hand weakly and warily at first. Again and again she licked his hand. He used both hands this time and brought her more and more water. She was drinking! he thought and almost laughed out loud. Even the cat in the rafters seemed relieved and happy. It purred loudly. Yes, she was drinking and she would get better, he knew it.

The wind beat against the barn and the night grew colder and colder. The boy ran the back of his hand along the deer's slender neck, soothing and comforting her. He adjusted the blanket around her and sat, cradling her head in his lap, until the sun came up and the other animals in the barn grew restless with the light. And once she was better, he thought, his mother would make a special collar for her with a bell on it. Everyone would know she was a pet and no hunter would shoot at her. A cold shiver traveled up his spine.

IT HAD BEEN his brother's idea to overturn the bathtub-sized, galvanized watering trough and to drag it across the fields to the pond. "It'll make a great boat, and all we've got to do is make some oars out of old scrap lumber," he had said.

"Pa won't like it," Trey warned.

"We'll bring it back before they get home and nobody will ever know."

So the boys struggled most of the morning, pulling and pushing the heavy trough to the water's edge. The cows followed behind, curious, or maybe worried about having to find water elsewhere for the rest of the day.

"Rub-a-dub-dub, I'll be right back with the grub," Troy said and trotted off up the hill to stock up on candy, fruit and peanut-butter sandwiches. Trey found two boards for oars, checked their fishing poles for tangles in the lines and quickly found a canful of worms in the rich sod under the poplar trees nearby.

"I christen thee Old Ironsides the Second," Troy

announced. He pushed the boat into the cold, spring-clear water. It rocked precariously back and forth.

The wind was cool, but the sun shone down warmly as they paddled out to the middle of the pond and nibbled at their picnic lunch. They tossed bread crumbs into the still, black water which immediately churned with hundreds of hungry shiners, three-inch-long bait fish whose prolific ancestors had been the survivors of so many ice-fishing expeditions up north on Lake Winnepesaukee.

Occasionally, a menacing pickerel would rise slowly from the depths and wait, like a submarine, just below the surface, surveying the swarming minnows. It would lie there, unnoticed by the other fish, then suddenly strike hard and fast at an unsuspecting shiner and disappear again. A great splash would clear the water for a moment. Only a few silver scales sparkled in the sunlight. Dinner had been served.

More bread crumbs would bring back the myriad of frantic, glistening minnows.

The boys were quick to pull their lines out of the water whenever a bullhead appeared. They hated catching one of the hideous, antennaed catfish that always swallowed the hook deep into its gullet and thrashed its spiny fins whenever they tried to dig it out.

By sundown, they had caught a half-dozen good-sized perch, sunfish and one lumbering bullhead. The fish, crowded together, gulped for air in a half-filled bucket that floated behind the boat, tethered by a piece of baling twine. Trey wanted to set the fish free.

"I've got a *big* one!" Troy shouted. His bamboo pole curved downward and tipped into the water. "It's a pickerel! A monster!" he yelled and, in his excitement, scurried about the boat on his knees.

"Watch out! You're going to sink us!" Trey shrieked. But his brother heard none of the warning. The boat tipped side to side. Water sloshed in over the edge and soaked their clothes. In an instant, the boat capsized and sank like a stone, out of sight, to the mucky bottom twenty feet below.

"Pa's going to *kill* us," Trey moaned to his brother as they dog-paddled their way toward shore. Troy laughed at their soggy state. He gripped his fishing pole tightly. Two apples and one slowly dissolving peanut-butter sandwich bobbed in their wake. The shiners moved in again for an afternoon snack and frothed the water with their frenzied eating.

"Swim for your life! *Piranha!*" Troy yelled, still laughing. Trey hightailed it to shore.

Troy's catch was indeed a prized pickerel, but Trey felt little call for celebration as he plodded toward the house. Water squirted through the eyelets of his sneakers and poured from his drenched clothing.

"I sunk the watering trough," Troy said in greeting his parents' return from a quiet day of shopping.

"We both did," confessed Trey as he stepped into the kitchen.

41

"I see," answered his father, not at all surprised. His mother covered a faint smile with her hand.

"What do you propose to do about it?" his father asked flatly.

"Well, I thought tomorrow you could bring the tractor down to the pond and Trey and I could tie a rope around the trough and you could pull it up." Troy sounded very calm and mature.

"And if we can't bring it up? What then?"

"I guess we'll have to pay you back," Trey suggested.

But the water was cold and murky and, even when the boys managed to find the sunken trough, they could find no place to which to tie the rope securely. Time and again they dove and rose to the surface, gasping for air and shivering from the cold water. Their father waited patiently on his idling tractor.

It took the twins the rest of the summer to pay back their father for the replacement watering trough, and only after they had convinced their mother to donate five dollars from her own savings.

Sometimes, on a bright summer's day, Trey could still see the metallic trough shining peacefully at the bottom of the pond.

"And good morning to you," his father said cheerfully. He leaned over the gate and tousled his son's hair. "How's our gracious guest?"

"She started drinking water, Pa," the boy returned.

42

"She's too weak to stand and reach the pail by herself, so I let her drink from my hands." The deer lay calm and nearly motionless. She followed the conversation with her mulelike ears.

"That's wonderful! Maybe old Freddy Coombs was right after all. Has she eaten anything yet?" He entered the nursery and dropped to one knee. He stroked the animal's neck. She seemed to like the attention. "Yes, you remember me, don't you, girl?"

"No, sir, she didn't touch her food all night."

"Well, the water's the most important thing for now. She lost a lot of blood yesterday. Did either of you get any sleep last night?"

"No. We talked, mostly." His father chuckled. "And I gave her a name, too," Trey added. "Tawny."

"Now, that's a right pretty name for a right pretty little lady, son."

"She likes it."

"I bet she does," said his father with a smile. He rose and turned to leave the pen. "How about giving me a hand with the livestock and then we'll see about putting some food into you and Tawny here. She'll be okay alone for a while. We'll give her a chance to sleep some."

"Yes, sir."

After the morning's milking and feeding, Trey returned to the house with a basketful of fresh eggs. The sunlight glared off the snow; it hurt his eyes. Maybe he would take a nap after breakfast, he thought.

43

"So what if Pa says we can't get a horse," Troy said suddenly, wrenching his brother from his thoughts.

"We can't afford one," Trey returned flatly.

"Look at all those cows." Troy motioned to the herd of Holsteins lying in the field under a cloudy August sky.

"So?"

"*So*, if we ever want to go for a ride, we've got a whole herd to pick from!"

"People don't ride cows," Trey said.

"How do you know? I bet they ride cows in China. And, what about all those rodeo riders?"

"They practically get *killed* on those big bulls!"

"Then, we'll ride a *small cow*," Troy answered logically. "Come on."

And the boys trotted over the closely shorn grass toward the peaceful, unsuspecting heifers.

"You go first," Troy said.

"Why me? It was your idea."

"Because I'm stronger than you are and I can hold her until you're ready." Trey thought that sounded vaguely sensible.

Nancy, a year-old Holstein, lay in the grass with her legs tucked under her, contentedly chewing her cud. She watched the boys' approach with her lazy brown eyes.

"See how easy this is going to be?" Troy said. "All you have to do is step on and wrap your arms around her neck. Simple."

44

"Yeah, sure." Trey sounded nervous.

Troy knelt before the trusting heifer and scratched her broad head. She liked that. "What are you waiting for? Get on her. She's not going to do anything. See? She's perfectly quiet."

"Right." Trey cautiously extended one leg over her back and climbed onto her barrel-shaped body. He leaned forward to wrap his arms around her neck.

Instantly, the heifer jumped to her feet and bolted across the field. Troy was thrown back, off balance. Trey pressed his chest tight against the animal's withers and hung on for dear life. The heifer bucked and swerved and kicked high into the air. He could hear Troy's laughter far behind him. "Watch out for the cow pies!" he called out and doubled over in laughter.

Up and down, right and left, back and forth Trey was jerked by the bucking heifer, but his hold was firm. Or so he thought. Suddenly, there was nothing but open space between himself and the ground. He sailed effortlessly over the cow's head, almost flying through the air. It seemed like hours that he hung there, surveying the landscape for a good place to land. And then, just as suddenly as he had taken off, Trey thudded against the soggy ground and tumbled, unhurt, over and over, head over heels. He could still hear his brother's laughter echoing over the field. Nancy trotted back to the herd as if nothing had ever happened.

"I told you to look out for the cow pies," Troy said while Trey peeled himself from the well-fertilized sod.

His clothes were streaked with manure and mud. He spat bits of grass out of his mouth.

"Pretty good, huh?" Trey asked his amused and approving brother.

"You did right fine for a young fella," Troy answered with a thick Texas drawl. "Right fine, indeed!"

The sun nestled down behind the pines and cast long streaks of shadows across the snow. He had slept through the entire day! Quickly, Trey dressed and left the house. He ran toward the barn. The two aluminum silos glowed eerily in the late-afternoon light.

"Your mother's in the back with Tawny," his father said, standing just inside the door. He held a large, tangled ball of hay at the end of a pitchfork. "Why don't you go have a look-see and say hello."

"She's fine, Trey," his mother said. And Trey peered eagerly over the nursery gate. Tawny lay in the straw, her forelegs tucked under her chest, her bandaged hind legs stretched across the floor. In spite of her awkward position, she appeared calm, comfortable and alert. She nibbled bits of bread contentedly.

Trey entered the pen and wrapped his arms around the doe's neck. He gave her a big hug and felt a great relief. His mother smiled at them. The danger had passed.

"You two make a mighty pretty picture," she said.

"Doc Sherburne is coming tomorrow, isn't he?" Trey asked.

"In the morning," his mother answered with a nod. "He'll be pleased to see how well she is recovering."

Adi wandered toward the nursery and mooed once at the doe inside. Tawny struggled to stand.

"Easy, girl," Trey said, but the deer paid no attention to him. She staggered onto her front legs and slowly dragged her hind legs under her. She wobbled like a newborn calf as she walked to the side of the pen. Trey stayed close to support her.

"Joe, look at this," his mother called. His father approached quietly and watched the doe stretch over the gate and reach toward the inquisitive calf. They touched noses, once, twice, then drew back in surprise. They stood and studied each other for a long time.

"Looks like Tawny has found herself a new friend," his father chuckled. Trey felt a twinge of jealousy for a moment.

"But we'll have to keep them separated until after Tawny's healed, won't we?" he asked his parents.

The veterinarian arrived the next morning in his yellow Jeep station wagon while Trey collected eggs in the chicken coop. He heard his father greet the man with a cheery, "Good morning!" Trey hurried to finish his chore.

"She looks very good, Joe. If you'd asked me two

days ago if she would be standing by now, I would have said, 'No way.' But look at her now! You two men do great work," said Doc Sherburne with a smile.

"That's Trey's work you're complimenting," Mr. Landry answered. "He spent the entire first night with her and got her drinking water. She's still weak and in pain, but she's well on the road to recovery."

"That she is. Now, let's have a look at those wounds." The doctor eased the doe onto her side and carefully cut away the bandages. Tawny seemed to know that he had come to help and showed no signs of fear or resistance.

The blood-stained bandages stuck to her legs and the doctor worked slowly to peel them away, being very careful not to reopen any of the gashes or hurt the trusting animal.

"She's mending pretty well, although she shouldn't do much walking until those stitches come out in a week or so." The boy watched as the wounds were cleaned and rebandaged and the doctor gave her one last injection of antibiotics.

"Call me if there are any complications. Otherwise, I'll be back this way the end of next week to see if I can remove those sutures. She should be fine until then." He shook Mr. Landry's hand and turned to leave the barn.

"Doc Sherburne," Trey called after him. He walked toward him with his hand outstretched. "Thanks, Doc," he said and shook the man's hand.

"My pleasure. But don't forget to thank yourself, too. You did as much as I did in keeping her alive." He walked out of the barn, humming the tune that played softly on the radio.

"Well, now, that was pretty good news," his father said with a smile. He placed his hand on his son's shoulder. "Real good news."

Trey felt proud and protective. Tawny sipped from her water bucket and looked into the boy's eyes.

He would take good care of her, he promised. Forever.

Part II

THE LANDRY FARM spread half a mile in all directions over the top of the highest hill in southern New Hampshire. In the fall, once the leaves had fallen from the trees, a man could stand in the fields and see the countryside rolling on forever. At night, the sky overhead was pitch black, but the horizons glowed from the city lights way in the distance: Nashua, Salem, Lowell. . . .

The state had long ago carved a one-acre clearing at the very peak of the hill and, in the middle of the clearing, was a fire lookout tower that stood on great, gray steel stilts above the bordering pines. And every April, Mr. Durkey, the watchman, chugged up the winding, muddy access road and moved into the tiny, two-roomed cabin at the base of the tower where he spent the spring, summer and autumn months alone. He was a wiry, funny old man who loved the solitude and the rustic life among the trees. It was his job to climb the long, winding stairs to the little house atop the scaffolding every morning at sunup and to survey the countryside for any telltale signs of smoke signaling a fire.

He liked the boys and they spent many summer afternoons with the old watchman in his tower. He told them stories of great forest fires he had seen and instructed them in the use of the many maps and charts and radios. For hours on end, the twins would pan over the country with binoculars, searching for the gray wisps of smoke that meant danger to all.

"What's that, Mr. Durkey?" one of the boys would ask. "Down there, by Gumpas Pond?" And Mr. Durkey would put down his whittling or his lunch or whatever else he was tinkering with and chart the coordinates on the table-top map. With great ceremony he would radio the fire warden's office for information.

"Mabel, this is Frank here. You got any permits issued around Gumpas Pond today? One of the Landry boys just spotted some smoke."

"Yes, Frank, Dr. Hinds is burning some brush on his land. Keep a close eye on it, though, the wind is picking up and the woods are pretty dry."

"Thanks, Mabel," Mr. Durkey said and shrugged his shoulders at the boys, who felt important and proud of their alertness.

On a clear day they could see all the way to Boston.

"That big domed thing is the John Hancock Building, boys," Mr. Durkey would say. "That's about fifty miles away as the crow flies. It's a big insurance company that pays people money whenever they die or their house burns down or their car gets wrecked."

It seemed to Trey that a company ought to pay people *not* to do any of those things, but he did not mention it aloud to the others.

Every year on the Fourth of July, Trey and his brother secretly climbed the stairs of the tower and sat on the uppermost platform beneath the elevated house and watched the fireworks from all over the area. The displays completely circled them from their vantage point. Every town and city had its own supply of fireworks and the boys set them off at the same time. A sudden flash would demand their attention and they counted, out loud, until they heard the echoing rumbles from the explosion.

"That one must have come from Salem, twenty miles away," Trey would say and then a burst of light behind them spun their heads toward Nashua or Pelham or Hudson Center. The fireworks looked like gigantic flowers in the sky: bursting, blossoming, rumbling and slowly dissolving into the night. The boys eagerly awaited the Grand Finale when the whole world erupted into vivid, brilliantly colored fire. Every color imaginable filled the sky from horizon to horizon, overlapping, blending, flashing, booming and fading with an electric excitement.

It was their favorite night of the year and, once the fireworks were over, the boys scrambled down the tower steps and short-cut through the forest to their house. And they waited, impatiently, for the next Fourth of July, which always seemed too far away.

But this April, winter held stubbornly onto the land. Snow covered the fields and piled high amid the shadows under the trees and along the sides of the roads. The pasture land was mushy and cold and the mud sucked at the cows' hooves as they ventured out into the fields. Daffodils, tulips and crocuses pushed their green shoots through the snow and reached for the sun in the southside flower gardens, and pussy willows, growing along the stream from the pond, burst their furry blossoms: the only signs of spring, which was taking its time arriving.

Even old Mr. Durkey, sitting in their kitchen, nursing a steaming cup of coffee, said he should have known better than to try to make it up the access road to the lookout tower. His rusted pickup truck sank axle-deep into the mud and had to be pulled out by the Landrys' tractor.

"You'd think by now, after all these years, I'd know enough to be patient and wait out the mud season." He winked once and smiled at Trey. "It's nice to be back in this neck of the woods. But you'll have to tell Troy that I won't be moving in until after next week."

The watchman had spent his winter, as usual, with his sister in Massachusetts. He had not heard of Troy's death. He listened, solemnly, as Mrs. Landry told him the old but still painful news. Trey tried not to listen.

The old man sat for a long time, silently hunched over his coffee cup; he shook his head slowly. "Maybe this year you and I can watch the fireworks," he said to the boy, finally breaking the long silence. Trey was not really surprised that Mr. Durkey knew, although he and his brother had never mentioned their annual adventure to the watchman, since the tower was off limits after sundown.

"Sure," Trey answered with an appreciative smile, but he doubted that he would ever again climb those tower stairs.

Tawny had recovered very well. Doc Sherburne, the veterinarian, had announced weeks ago that she was as healthy as he was and stopped checking in on her as soon as the bandages had been removed once and for all. Her legs were scarred, and some of the hair probably would never grow back completely, but she was happily up and about and she grew bolder every day. She limped slightly when she walked.

Over the remaining winter weeks, Tawny grew quite accustomed to farm life and at milking time she followed Trey and his father around the barn or trotted after Adi into the nursery where they watched the scurryings of their keepers. Tawny even learned to drink from the watering bowls and to open the heavy lid of the grain bin at night when no one was there to stop her. A handy snap latch was used to foil her nightly raids and she angrily rattled the latch with

57

her nose, but Tawny could not have her own way *all* the time.

Every morning she waited by the door for Trey's arrival and merrily scampered off ahead, as if she had a secret to show him.

The chickens worried her, though. She did not know what to make of the nervously squawking hens and kept a safe distance from them. She thumped her hoof against the floor whenever Trey entered the coop, almost as a warning for him to be careful.

And, one day, a photographer from the local newspaper arrived and asked to speak with Trey. He and the boy chatted for an hour about Tawny and her new life on the Landry farm. The doe circled them slowly as they talked in the barn, keeping a wary eye on the stranger's complicated photographic equipment. The man took notes on a small pad as Trey spoke. And right before he left, the man took two pictures of the boy and his deer. Tawny flinched from the bright, sudden burst of light and shook her head, as if she were trying to remove the spots in her eyes.

Two days later, a picture of Tawny and Trey appeared in the Saturday edition with a story of the doe's rescue from the murderous pack of dogs. Trey clipped the article from the newspaper and taped it to the wall over his desk. It had a small corner missing where Tawny had tried to eat the scrap of paper when the boy showed it to her.

Both Trey and the doe enjoyed the sudden rush of

attention. Friends and neighbors, having read the article, frequently stopped by the farm to meet the doe and to congratulate Trey on his wonderful pet. Time and again, Trey was asked to retell the story of Tawny's rescue and recovery which he did obligingly, being careful not to exaggerate his role in saving the doe's life.

And out of all his classmates, only Joel Ducharme was invited to the farm to see Tawny. Every day, the two boys ate their lunch together, sitting at a small table in the cafeteria and talking about next year's basketball season and school work. They never mentioned Troy and Trey decided that was just as well. He knew how close Joel and his brother had been and that Troy's death had come almost as hard for Joel as it had for himself. Joel will talk about Troy when he wants to, Trey thought.

They rode the bus up the hill to the Landry farm and headed straight for the barn. Tawny took to Joel right away. Trey carefully shook out a portion of hay for the deer to eat, but she would accept only the hay Joel offered to her from his hand.

"She's beautiful, Trey," Joel said. Tawny nuzzled his hand. "Troy would have been proud of her."

"Yes, he would," Trey returned.

"And I bet Troy would have bragged all over school about how you saved her."

Trey smiled.

59

Three days after Joel's visit to the farm, Trey was asked to write a special piece for his school newspaper about Tawny and his life with her. He worked on the story for the better part of a week and, finally, when it was finished, he realized that he had written mostly about hunters—people and animals—and about how carelessly they ravaged the countryside. His teacher called it an essay and read it out loud to the whole class.

But, in spite of her growing boldness and all the attention paid her, Tawny refused to venture outside the barn. Whenever the weather was seasonably warm, Trey led the doe to the open barn door and stepped outside. "Come on, Tawny," he coaxed, but she would go no farther than the door. Inquisitively, she stuck her head out and looked about, but never would she step into the sun. She seemed not to understand the boy's urgings. Eventually, Tawny grew tired of the game and returned to her pen where she was safe and warm and where there was always plenty to eat. Trey wished that just once the doe would follow him into the pasture. There were so many things he wanted to show her.

By mid-April, the ice on the pond turned slushy white and began to melt around the edges. Slowly, the ice became smaller and smaller and, like a floating island, drifted from one bank to the other with the wind. The water level grew higher every day, swelling from the run-off of the melting snow. The pond reached the bases of the poplar trees; they showed faint signs of developing shoots and tender buds. The overflow gushed through the run-off culvert and rushed down the rocky stream through the fields.

Wearing his green rubber boots with yellow soles, Trey followed the stream, building little dams with rocks and soggy leaves. The water was bitter cold and as clear as crystal; it built up over the dams and gurgled on down the stream. He built a tiny raft made of sticks and watched it spin crazily around and around, trapped in a miniature whirlpool. As he opened his little dam, the water rushed forward. He stood alone, watching the tiny boat slide over the smooth rocks, downstream, out of sight.

A cold, misting rain began to fall from the low-hanging clouds. Fog rolled out of the forest and over the field. He let the icy water run over his feet. He felt hollow and alone. Troy could have made this a special day, he thought.

The rain fell harder and pelted against the barn's tin roof. It was a soothing sound that grew louder as the boy climbed the ladder into the hayloft. From the open trap door he could see Tawny below him, asleep on the straw in her pen. He did not wish to disturb her. Quietly, he settled himself between the scratchy bales of hay and pulled his damp jacket close under his chin. He felt safe and secure and hidden. The rain would turn to snow during the night, he thought before he fell into a sound sleep.

61

"Well, Trey, how does it feel being a celebrity?" asked Mrs. Richardson, the minister's wife, at the Wednesday night potluck supper. It was the first time since Troy's funeral that the woman had spoken to him.

"Fine," answered the boy, a bit shyly. He held in his hands a paper plate, almost overflowing with helpings of potato salad, baked beans, slices of ham and turkey and corn bread. The plate grew limper as he held it.

Immediately, Trey was crowded by townspeople asking all sorts of questions about himself and Tawny. How was she recovering? Did he think she would ever walk without a limp? What did he feed her? Did Tawny get along with the other animals on the farm? Was she afraid of strangers? Did he have any pictures of the doe? Could Miss Abbott bring her third-grade class up to the farm to meet her? How did Trey still find the time to help out with all the other chores? . . . Trey answered each and every one of the questions as thoroughly as he could. He was beginning to think that he would never be able to eat his meal. The now-soggy paper plate threatened to dissolve in his hands.

"When are you going to set her free?" asked old Mrs. Clara Johnson. Suddenly, Trey heard no other question. The other voices around him seemed to fade away. He stammered, but could not think of a way to answer the woman. He stared at her faded cotton dress. He had never before thought of setting Tawny free.

"How are those three kittens we gave you, Mrs. Johnson?" he asked, trying desperately to change the subject. He did not hear her answer. He did not want to talk to anyone any more. He did not want to eat his supper. He wanted to go home.

Quietly, Trey excused himself from the crowd of people and walked through the long room toward the exit. He left his plate of food on the last table and walked outside.

Away from the scrambled voices and faces, away from the rich smells and the laughter and the gossip, Trey climbed into the back seat of the family car and waited for his parents' return.

It wasn't fair, he thought. It just wasn't fair.

THE WARM DAYS and freezing, late-April nights signaled the start of the sugar maple season. In the morning, Trey and his father loaded the flat-bed trailer behind the tractor with wooden mallets, a pailful of tubular taps, two heavy hand drills and two dozen galvanized buckets. They rolled over the field, up the rise, toward the stand of maple trees, or sugar bushes as they are called. It was the first time Trey had approached the forest since the night his brother died. He was glad his father was with him.

Carefully, they selected the best maples for tapping and, depending on the size and age of the tree, decided how many holes were to be drilled into the sapwood. Trey sunk the drill bit into the pulpy bark. He leaned into the tree and slowly cranked the bit brace around and around. It made a scraping noise. The wet wood fell to the ground in clumps and curls as the drill dug farther into the sapwood. Once the hole was just deep enough, the boy sunk a hollow tube into the tree trunk with a few taps of his mallet. Special sugaring buckets were hung from the spigots: metal pails with "roofs" over their tops to keep out the rain and snow.

And once the sun climbed higher into the sky and warmed the earth below, the thin "sweet water sap" rose slowly from the roots toward the swelling buds on the branches. *Pink-pink-pink,* the sugar sap hit the bottoms of the empty buckets in painfully slow drops.

The boy sampled the clear sap on his finger. It tasted weak and woody, not at all like it would once all the collected sap was boiled down into a rich, amber syrup. To Trey, the hardest part of sugaring was the waiting: waiting for exactly the right time of year, waiting for the buckets to fill drop by drop, and waiting for the sap—all twelve gallons of it—to boil slowly down into three quarts of the precious maple syrup.

A huge copper kettle covered the stove and boiled violently, filling the kitchen with heavy, sweet steam and coating the windows with condensing water. The first two weeks' worth of sap turned thicker and darker.

"Goodness, it's like a steam bath in here," his mother said and wiped down the window by the sink with a towel. Trey stepped out the swinging screen door and watched the steam escape from the house to join the clouds high overhead.

"Listen," he said, searching the sky.

Way in the distance, Trey heard the steady *onk-onk-onk* of geese approaching.

"That means spring is finally here to stay," his

mother said. "Ike and Mamie are coming north." Trey smiled and looked southward.

High above the trees, just this side of the hill, he saw two Canadian geese flying closer and closer, their calls growing louder and louder. Every year, the same pair of geese stopped off at the Landrys' pond and visited for one week before they continued on their way. "They look like flying footballs," Troy had said once, and Trey always laughed whenever he saw them silhouetted against the sky.

Trey ran down the hill and hid among the poplars and watched the ritual through tiny feathers of soft green leaves. The huge, black-and-gray birds circled the pond again and again; their trumpeting became more excited. Their powerful wings stroked the air gracefully as they flew in tandem, wing tip to wing tip, banking perfectly together at every turn. And then Ike, the brave male, dropped toward the water. He glided like a great and beautiful kite toward the pond's choppy surface, webbed feet extended out in front of his body like skis. He touched down lightly and skimmed the water, skating over the surface, gradually settling comfortably into the frigid water at the edge of the remaining ice mass. Only then did he fold his wings to his sides. He flicked his tail side to side.

Mamie, the female, continued to circle the pond and onk-ed loudly as her mate surveyed their rest spot for any signs of danger. Finally, she too dropped toward the pond. So easily she floated down and down.

But, somehow, she misjudged her landing and skidded over the ice with a frantic back-pedaling of her wings. She splashed into the water at the bigger male's side. Ike acted as if nothing unusual had happened. Trey thought that very kind of him.

The two birds paddled idly around the pond, searching for the right place to build their temporary nest. Trey knew they would decide to settle among the dried cat-o'-nine-tails on the far bank. They always nested there.

The ringing of the telephone shattered the silence over lunch. His father answered. Trey held his sandwich in both hands, not daring to eat. Something was wrong.

"Oh, hello, Frank. How are you?" he heard his father say. The watchman never called the house, Trey thought.

Quickly, his father slammed down the receiver and grabbed his coat. He ran toward the back door. "Come with me!" he called. Trey and his mother scrambled from the table in pursuit.

Thick gray smoke poured from the barn doors. The terrified moos of the cows inside filled the air. Why had they not heard the commotion before? Trey wondered as he ran toward the barn. Tawny! Tawny was inside!

His father reached the sliding doors before Trey and his mother did. He threw them open wide. "Get the animals outside!" he hollered and choked from the smoke. Trey unrolled his turtleneck sweater over his nose and mouth. His mother splashed water from a puddle over her clothing before she entered the barn.

Trey's eyes burned from the smoke. His lungs ached with each breath. Flames lapped across the front of the building and reached toward the hayloft above. His father tugged at the hose from the milk room and opened it on the burning walls and ceiling.

Trey ran among the panicked cows, unlatching their stanchions and shooing them toward the only exit from the barn, the gaping, opened space surrounded by fire. He called frantically for the doe.

He and his mother worked quickly, freeing the animals, but they refused to approach the flames. The cows climbed over one another and tried to turn back into the smoke-filled barn. His mother tugged at one cow by its horns and covered its eyes with her arm. If one made it outside, the others would follow. Trey helped her, slapping and pushing on the animal's hindquarters until it stumbled into the fresh air.

His father doused the burning walls, calling out instructions to his wife and son. The cows stampeded out of the barn in one mass, knocking one of the sliding doors from its track and dashing it to the ground.

Tawny was not in her pen! Trey searched through blinding smoke for the doe. He called her again and again, but she did not show herself. Maybe she already escaped, he thought, and turned to run back toward the doors. He tripped over her trembling body, half-buried in the straw. He crawled to her on his hands and knees. The air was cooler and fresher close to the floor. Tawny had instinctively done the right thing.

"Come on, girl," he begged, pulling at her to stand. But she would not move. "Get up, Tawny. *Please!*" But the doe refused to budge. The fire crackled and popped, fanned by the fresh air from the open doors. Quickly, the boy wrapped his arms around the doe and struggled to stand. She kicked and tried to wriggle free, but Trey held firm. He staggered through the barn, through the fiery exit and into the barnyard. He heard the sirens of the fire engines coming up the road. Tawny wrenched free and tumbled to the ground.

The boy left the doe among the huddled, mooing cows and ran back inside to help his mother and father.

"They're coming up the road," Trey told them. His father nodded to the boy.

"The chickens!" his mother yelled.

"They're at the other end of the building; they'll be all right," Trey answered. His hair was singed and tears poured down his cheeks. The heat from the fire was tremendous, but he continued to splash buckets full of water onto the flames. His mother filled the empty pails from the milk room and handed them back to her son. His father sprayed the ceiling, trying to keep the flames out of the hayloft.

Through the doors, Trey saw the fire engines

creeping through the herd of cows. Help had arrived. Firemen equipped with portable "Indian tanks" moved ahead of the emergency vehicles. They entered the barn and immediately began spraying the fire from the pressurized water tanks on their backs. One man climbed into the hayloft with the heavy tank over his shoulder. More men entered the barn dragging a fire hose from the pump truck and directed the torrents of water on the building's front wall.

In a matter of minutes, the fire was out. Charred and soggy wood smoldered and popped. Murky water poured from the ceiling and down the walls, sliding into ashen-mucky puddles on the floor. It was quiet again and the smoke slowly cleared. A musty, acrid odor remained.

"Looks like that's the culprit," said the fire chief. He pointed at the charred remains of the old radio.

"Guess the poor old thing decided to go out with a bang!" his father answered, half-jokingly. Trey could see the relief in his face.

The firemen began coiling the long, canvas-covered fire hoses and stowing their equipment. Mrs. Landry fetched a pot of fresh coffee to serve them. The men relaxed and joked with the boy's father, happy to have prevented a tragedy. Even the cows had settled down; they circled the fire engines, curious and friendly.

But Tawny was nowhere in sight. Trey studied her tiny hoof prints in the soft earth. They led away from the barn, down the hill, to the edge of the pond. She stood among the poplars and watched the noisy geese as they paddled closer and closer.

Hhhhhhh! the aggressive male hissed viciously, his wings extended threateningly. He made a sound like air escaping from an inner tube. *Hhhhhhh!* he hissed again and lumbered out of the water toward the doe. His neck looked like a great serpent. *Clup-clup.* He snapped at the deer with his saw-toothed bill.

Trey knew the gander meant business. He had heard stories of geese severely wounding dogs and even men with the pounding of their powerful wings. And Ike was not pleased by Tawny's sudden intrusion; he was intent on protecting his mate and his territory.

Tawny was confused and curious, but not yet frightened by the big goose. She moved a little closer. The gander lunged forward, thrashing his wings and wildly snapping his bill. Trey stepped between Ike and the doe. His father had told him what to do in moments like this; he hoped he was right. The boy hunched forward and stretched his arms out wide. Trey hissed back at the gander and looked into his eyes.

It worked. The bird stopped in mid-attack and studied the boy with a cock of its head. A stand-off.

Slowly, the goose tucked its wings to its sides and, with a ruffle of feathers and a flutter of his tail, he turned and padded back to the water's edge.

Playfully, Tawny nudged Trey's side.

"Ike isn't very friendly, girl. You should be more careful when he's around," the boy lectured. Tawny rose on her hind legs, turned and pranced away, inviting the boy to chase after her. They ran together over the field, moving in a lazy arc toward the barn.

Like a puppy she played, hopping and scampering this way and that, bouncing high into the air. Almost as if she were only just remembering her speed and graceful agility, Tawny sprinted over the pasture. Trey ran after her, but was easily outrun by the doe. "Showoff!" he called out. Tawny darted back to his side, then shot off in another direction. At last he had a companion, he thought. No longer afraid to venture outside, Tawny could be shown all of Trey's favorite haunts and secret hiding places. He wondered what she might be able to show him, too.

The firemen had departed by the time Trey and the doe returned to the barn. The cows, obviously having forgotten the dangers the building once held for them, moved quietly back into their stanchions on their own. It was clean-up time.

After escorting the deer back to her pen, Trey retrieved the long, coarse-bristled push broom from the milk room and began sweeping the gray-muddy water out the door. He heard his father in the loft, lugging soggy bales of hay down to be used for the night's feeding. He knew the bales had to be opened quickly. Left alone, the compressed wet hay would rot and generate enough heat possibly to start another fire by spontaneous combustion. Most of the front wall and the door frame would have to be replaced, and maybe even some of the boards in the ceiling, he thought. Trey pushed more water toward the door. But the major repairs to the damaged walls would be a long time coming. They would have to wait until after planting season was over.

ON THE DAY Trey and his brother were born, their father planted a tiny crab-apple sapling in the yard, right beside the front door. Soon it outgrew its need for supportive wires and stakes and now it stood many times taller than the boy. For one week its spring-swollen buds hinted at their surprise of color and, in one night, the blossoms burst forth all together. The sweet, pink-flower scent filled the morning air and, carried by the breeze, drifted into his room. Tiny soft petals fluttered to the ground.

Trey stood beneath the beautiful tree and admired it in the morning light. A tiny emerald-throated hum-mingbird hovered on invisible wings and darted among the blossoms, dipping its needle beak into the flowers. It seemed to enjoy its breakfast of sweet nectar and boldly flew around the boy's head once or twice.

Carefully, Trey snapped a small branch from a lower limb and carried it into the kitchen where Mrs. Landry busied herself with preparations for breakfast.

"Happy Mother's Day!" he said and presented the blossom-filled bough to his mother with a hug and a kiss. With Troy gone, did he have to try doubly hard to fulfill his mother's hopes for him? he wondered.

They held each other for a long time. And he thought, just for a moment, that his mother was crying.

The plow was held above the ground by the tractor's hydraulic three-point hitch. Its three blades, polished by so many years' work, shone in the sun. With a muffled hiss, it dropped stiffly to the ground and the tractor groaned as it pulled away. The blades bit hard into the richly fertilized earth. As the tractor picked up speed, it moved effortlessly over the long field. The plow sliced into the ground and casually flipped the sod over into long, straight rows. Robins swooped and scurried across the freshly overturned earth, sometimes stopping suddenly to tug mercilessly at a surprised worm that held on for dear life.

Trey stood at the edge of the field, watching his father pilot the tractor and wondering if he would ever learn to keep the plow furrows as straight. Both he and his brother had learned to drive at the age of eight. Patiently, their father had taught them the intricacies of clutching and shifting, braking and accelerating. They practiced their driving skills in the early evening after their chores were finished. They had to sit on a Sears and Roebuck catalogue to see over the dashboard of the pickup truck as they bounced over the fields. Learning to drive had been fun for the boys, although in a farming community like theirs, driving at such an early age was not unusual. Some kids their age even owned their very own "field cars" to hot-rod around in. Had Troy not gotten carried away last year and driven the tractor through the garage door, Trey might be piloting it right now, he thought.

Tawny lay nearby, peacefully nibbling on a blade of grass that dangled from her mouth. Two gray mourning doves circled the field. They moved perfectly together, as if tethered by an invisible line.

"Hey, daydreamer, are we going to finish this job?" his mother asked. The two were repairing the bordering barbed-wire fence. Every winter, heavy snowdrifts wreaked havoc with the fences, knocking down posts and stretching the wire until it was limp and useless.

"Sorry," Trey answered, "I was watching Pa."

"Your time at the wheel will come soon enough," his mother said. She knew what he had been thinking.

Trey picked up his bent-claw hammer and fit a wire barb between its tines. He tugged at the wire and leaned away from it, pulling it as tight as a guitar string. His mother used a U-shaped nail to attach it to the post.

His father turned his tractor around at the far end of the field and headed back toward them. The plow glanced off and scraped against a shallow shelf of granite.

"Uh! I hate that noise," his mother said, placing her hands over her ears. "It always reminds me of someone dragging his fingernails over a blackboard."

Trey chuckled. "You say that every year."

He picked up the heavy sledgehammer and thumped the top of a wobbly post. The head of the stake splintered and mashed down as it sunk deeper into the ground. "There, that should do it," said the boy, testing the post. "Solid as a rock."

"Hey!" his father called over the noise of the working tractor engine from the middle of the field. He pointed into the air. The two geese, Ike and Mamie, their great wings beating into the wind, rose slowly from the pond and circled it once before heading northward. The boy and his mother waved after them. "See you next year," Trey called happily. Gradually, the birds' rhythmic onk-onking faded away.

"I thought after their run-in with Tawny that they would leave early. But they stayed around an extra week," said the boy.

"Now that Tawny's no longer afraid to leave the barn and is spending so much time outdoors, I think we should make a collar for her so that everyone will know she's a pet," his mother said.

"Okay," answered the boy, secretly happy that they were talking about keeping her.

As if on cue, Tawny approached the boy and his mother. They stopped their work momentarily and stroked the animal's neck. Trey ran his hand over her back and swatted her rump. "Scoot, now. We've got work to do. We'll play later," he said and Tawny obligingly left them to settle herself beneath an old oak tree. She sighed, impatient for the work to be over.

The day's work was completed before sundown. The boy's parents rode back toward the house on the tractor. Tawny and Trey stayed behind and wandered toward the neighboring orchard.

"Oh, Tawny, not you, too!" Trey shouted. The doe swallowed a mouthful of poison ivy. Over the years, Trey had grown accustomed to seeing the cows gorge themselves on the shiny, three-leaved plants. He had even stopped worrying whether or not their milk was safe to drink. But the boy's stomach began to knot up as he watched Tawny devour the toxic leaves. The thought of bringing a piece of poison ivy anywhere near his mouth made his skin crawl.

"Get out of there," he ordered. Tawny waded through the patch of lush, ground-hugging foliage. He would have to remember to hose her down when they got back to the barn, he thought. Otherwise, his hands would soon be covered with itchy blisters.

"I suppose it's a good thing you're not allergic to that stuff," he said. "How would you scratch yourself?" Tawny moved toward the bordering stand of young pines.

The apple blossoms had already gone by and the faded flower petals covered the ground like snow. The sweet fragrance remained. Tawny scampered among the trees and Trey tried not to notice when she nibbled an occasional bud or shoot from a low-hanging limb. She looked so pretty in the setting, he thought: happy, at home.

Home! He had almost forgotten. "Come on, girl!" he called. "It's milking time and I'm late."

They raced each other back to the barn.

The wind picked up from the north. It was a cold, gusty wind that slammed against the house and made for an exceptionally cozy evening by the fire in the living room. Trey sat in his favorite overstuffed chair with his feet propped on the ottoman. His parents sat close by on the couch. His mother fashioned a new collar for Tawny from an old red leather belt that had belonged to his brother. His father flipped through the pages of a *Life* magazine that had arrived in the day's mail. There were rumors that Alaska was about to become a state. Number forty-nine, Trey thought. He wondered if there was any mention of it in his father's magazine. He tried to imagine how the stars on the new flag would be arranged. It's still winter in Alaska, he thought, and snuggled down into his chair.

A large mirror hung on the far wall of the living room. Trey studied its richly carved frame and watched the reflected scene inside. It was a pleasant, peaceful picture of his family, Trey thought.

Six months, he thought. Troy had been dead for half a year. Yet Trey still did not believe his brother was gone. Not really. In his dreams, he still shared his adventures with his twin. Sometimes, he found himself wondering where Troy was, why he had not come home. And every once in a while, Trey surprised himself by thinking it was his brother's reflection that stared back at him in the mirror. Like now, Trey thought.

There he was in the glass. There *they* were. The same blond hair, the same blue eyes, the same pencil-line space between the front teeth. Identical, but different, somehow. They had shared the same clothes, the same food, pondered the same questions and learned the same things.

It was his own face and his brother's he saw every morning. Together, they formed one whole person. Would it always be like this? he asked himself.

"There, it's done," announced his mother, holding up the new collar. A tiny silver bell attached to its buckle rang merrily. "Think she'll like it?"

"I'm going to put it on her right now," Trey said. He ran to the barn with the collar in his hand.

At first, Tawny was confused by the slight tightness around her neck. For a while, she walked around her pen shaking her head and rubbing herself against the wall, trying to remove the collar. But eventually she realized the collar meant her no harm and settled into the idea of wearing it.

"I think it looks nice," the boy said. "And now, even strangers will know that you're a member of the family."

He returned to the house to tell his parents the news. He forgot to lock the nursery gate when he left.

It was a muted, distant sound that worked its way into his dream. But, as he drifted toward awakening, the sounds in the house grew louder and louder. A sudden smash and clatter yanked him completely from his sleep. The kitchen! he thought, and jumped from his bed.

Crash!-crash!-crash!-crash! He ran to the back of the house, rubbing his eyes into focus.

Trey snapped on the kitchen light. The room was a shambles! Chairs were overturned, pots and pans were knocked from their hooks on the wall, the floor was covered with broken glass.

In the pantry, the lower shelf had collapsed and dozens of canning jars had slid to the kitchen floor and shattered, one at a time, into a gooey, sticky, oozing mess of fruit, syrup, vegetables and broken glass. He watched as one last canning jar rolled on its side to the edge of the counter.

Splat! It hit the floor.

The huge flour bin had been knocked over and its contents covered the room from corner to corner.

And there she stood, amid the rubble, covered ghostly-white with flour.

"Tawny!" his mother screamed from behind him. She clutched her bathrobe around her shoulders.

"Get her back to the barn, son," his father said

sternly. "And get yourself right back here and help me clean up this mess."

"Boy, Tawny, we're in for it now," said the boy, tugging at the doe's collar. Reluctantly, she followed beside him. The white flour on her coat blew off her body like smoke. "That was really dumb."

"There's a man coming tomorrow that I want you to meet," his father said. He and the boy worked together sweeping up the rubble from Tawny's midnight raid. Trey slathered the tacky floor with a mop. "His name is Leon French and he works at the Wild Animal Farm in Hudson."

"Why?" Trey asked.

"Because he and I have spoken on the phone about his letting Tawny move in there." His father's words hit him like a slap across the face. Trey could feel the tears building up in his eyes.

"She's a wild animal, son, and she has to be treated like one."

"No, she isn't!" Trey protested. "She's just like a member of the family."

"She's *tame* is all, but she still has all those instincts in her that don't set well with people and domesticated animals. It isn't fair to her to think we're going to change her."

Trey did not answer his father. He stared at the broken chunks of glass at his feet.

"Tawny isn't like Adi or the other cows," his father continued. "She doesn't know what it's like to be penned in. She jumps over fences." Trey knew what was coming next. "Already she's killed off three of the apple-tree saplings we set out last fall. She doesn't understand what's off limits and what isn't."

"She could learn, Pa!" Trey cried.

"It's not our place to force her to do anything. That would destroy her spirit, you know that." There was a long silence which Trey did not want to break. He wanted to go to bed. Maybe his father would feel differently in the morning, he thought.

"Mr. French isn't coming up here tomorrow to take Tawny away. I just want you to hear him out and to decide on your own what is best for Tawny."

"Yes, sir," answered the boy.

"So, THIS is the Trey Landry I've read so much about in the papers." Mr. French extended his hand to the boy in greeting. "You've done a wonderful thing with that doe of yours, keeping her alive and helping her get well and all." The man had a friendly, open face and a pleasant voice, not at all what Trey had expected. It was going to be hard for the boy not to like him.

"May I meet Tawny?" the man asked.

"Sure," Trey answered. "She's in the barn with Pa." The boy led the way and listened to the man's cheerful small talk.

"She's a pretty one, Joe," Mr. French said. He stood in the nursery stall with the deer and ran his hand over her back. "She'll fit in just fine with the rest of the herd at the Animal Farm."

"Well, Leon, like I explained to you on the phone, whether or not Tawny is moved over there has a lot to do with what Trey decides. She's his doe."

The visitor closed the gate behind him and sat down on a convenient bale of hay close to where the boy stood. Trey braced himself.

"You've been to our Wild Animal Farm before, haven't you, Trey?"

"Yes, sir." Trey did not mention that his annual visit to the Farm was one of his favorite activities.

"Then you've seen for yourself what good care we take of all our animals?"

"Yes, sir."

"Natural settings, lots of fresh air and sunlight. . . ."

"Yes, sir."

"Tawny would live with fifteen other white-tailed deer, just like her, in a huge fenced-in area." The boy had visited them many times. "Why, I bet there's almost a whole acre there for her to run around in." The heavily wooded plot was barren, overgrazed, Trey thought. The deer lived on hay and grain.

"We've got one hundred and eighty-five acres for her here, sir," Trey answered. Mr. French cleared his throat and looked to the boy's father.

"But you know as well as your father and I that she can't roam free on the farm. She'd get into the crops and the new trees you set out last fall. . . ."

Trey looked squarely at his father, angry at him for having told the stranger about the new apple trees.

"And that one acre she'd be on with the other deer is protected by a ten-foot-high chain-link fence. Nothing can get in and bother her. She'll have plenty of good food and there's a freshwater stream that runs on the land. And she'll be fed plenty of biscuits from the tourists who come to visit. That doesn't sound like a bad life, does it?" Trey knew that most of the deer on the Animal Farm had been born in captivity. They knew no other way.

"No, sir," Trey answered.

"So, what do you say?" Mr. French looked pleased. Trey thought for a moment. Tawny was different from those deer. She was born wild. She knew a better life.

"No, sir," he said.

"What?"

"No, sir. I don't want Tawny in your animal farm."

"But why?" his father asked.

"I could make special arrangements for you to come and visit her any time you like. Free of charge," Mr. French persisted.

"Tawny is a wild animal," Trey said. He turned and pointed at his father. "You told me that, Pa. You said that she doesn't understand about fences and what's off limits and what isn't. Tawny needs places where she can run free and be alone, away from people and not just stuck in a cage where people can come and take her picture and feed her crackers."

"Let's be reasonable about this, son," the man said.

"I am being reasonable," Trey answered flatly. "Tawny should be free to come and go as she pleases, just like the rest of us." He turned and ran from the barn.

There was no mention of the day's confrontation at the dinner table that night. Trey and his parents ate their meal in silence.

His grandfather used to say, "Any stranger that travels all the way up this hill more than once deserves a good eyeing." And Trey wished his parents were home when the same wood-paneled station wagon with out-of-state license plates circled the driveway for the third time. The boy peered through the sheer living-room curtains; he watched the driver closely.

The man wore a black "city coat" and dark glasses. Trey thought the stranger to be about the same age as his father. The driver did not see the boy. His eyes remained fixed upon Tawny as she browsed quietly on the front lawn.

The doe paid no attention to the trespasser. She strolled casually across the front of the house, and her bell rang softly with each step. She stopped, briefly, in front of the window where Trey stood and then rounded the corner, out of Trey's line of vision. Surely that man knows Tawny is a pet, the boy reassured himself. His eyes were riveted to the driver in the car. The house was completely silent, almost as if it were holding its breath. Trey heard the faint ringing of Tawny's bell in the back yard.

The car stopped. And then it happened. The stranger reached slowly into the back seat and pulled out a gleaming new pump-action shotgun. He opened the door to step out.

Frantically, Trey ran to the front door and threw it open. "You're trespassing on private property, mister," Trey yelled.

The man stopped, momentarily surprised to find anyone at home, but he was not intimidated by the boy's voice. "Stay in the house, sonny, and nobody will get hurt. I'll only be a minute." The man continued across the front lawn and pumped his shotgun once. It was ready to fire.

Trey ran through the house, blindly knocking over an end table in the living room, and pulled his father's Winchester from its rack on the wall. He hurried into the kitchen, spilled a box of cartridges on the table and fumbled with the shells to load the rifle. He saw Tawny through the window.

As he reached the back door he saw the man rounding the far corner of the house, shotgun raised and ready. He was stalking the doe.

"I *said*, you're on private property!" Trey screamed through the screen door. Tawny perked up her ears. She knew there was danger nearby. The man did not answer. He stared coldly at the doe. With a flick of her tail, Tawny bolted toward the other side of the house. The hunter snapped his gun to his shoulder and aimed.

Trey kicked open the back door.

A single shot shattered the afternoon quiet. Like thunder, it echoed and rumbled over the hills. Trey felt his heart pounding in his ears. His face flushed and his hands tingled electrically. Tawny had vanished and everything else seemed frozen in space.

He had shot high, over the man's head. But this time Trey leveled the rifle squarely at the man's chest. He fought back the urge to fire again.

"If you don't set that gun on the ground and walk away, I promise you'll never make it back to Connecticut." Trey hissed the words through clenched teeth.

The man, frozen with fear, turned pale and trembled visibly. Slowly, he set the shotgun on the grass and stepped away, his hands raised to his shoulders.

Trey walked toward the trespasser. "Don't shoot," the man pleaded. Trey motioned with the rifle barrel and prodded the man's stomach. "Move," he said. He escorted the man back to his car, ignoring his frightened babbling. Perspiration poured down the intruder's face; his thin hair stuck, damp and limp, to his forehead.

Trey stopped beside the station wagon. "Get in," he ordered. The man obeyed. "Get out of here and don't come back." The car roared into life and shuddered out of the driveway, kicking up stones in its wake. Trey stood in the middle of the road and watched as the car hurried down the hill, out of sight. He stood there until the dust in the road had settled and the quiet returned to the air.

Tawny's tinny bell sounded in the distance. Trey turned to watch her trot merrily toward him. Suddenly, he noticed a loud ringing in his ears. His shoulder ached from the kick of the rifle, his arms felt heavy and weak. He thought his legs were about to collapse under him. Trey knelt on the lawn and set the

89

rifle down beside him. Tawny approached and nuzzled his chest. He wrapped his arms around her neck and pressed his cheek against her. She felt warm and relaxed. "That was a close one," the boy said. He felt exhausted.

Tawny licked the salty sweat from his hands.

"You did the right thing, son. I'm proud of you," his father reassured. The shotgun lay, unloaded, on the kitchen table. His mother touched his shoulder lightly.

"Most hunters are good, responsible people. We need them to keep the deer population in check so the others don't starve in the winter. But some hunters —the bad apples—think they're God Himself as soon as they get a gun in their hands. They think they have a right to go wherever they want, whenever they want, and to shoot at anything that moves." Trey remembered the time he saw a hunter stopped by state police on the highway. A full-grown collie was strapped to the hood of his car: his prize kill of the day.

"I'll call Ralph in the morning and see if he knows anyone in town who wants a new shotgun," his father said. "I don't think this one's ever been fired." The town's police chief had an arsenal of weapons, confiscated from irresponsible hunters.

"What do you plan to do?" his father asked. Trey knew he was talking about the doe.

A deer should be free to roam, he thought. If Tawny were back in the wild she, like the other deer, would find plenty of food away from the farm, away from people. She would learn to be wary of men with guns and she would find safety in the heavily-wooded high ground where she could bear her young. Yes, she would be safe at the animal farm, he told himself. Nothing would threaten her again. But Tawny came from a different world. Moving her there would destroy her spirit. She would be safe, but she would no longer be Tawny. She needed to be free and he would help her to go back to the life for which she was born.

"Teach her," Trey answered at last.

"I thought we already agreed last week before Mr. French came here that it wouldn't be fair to try to teach Tawny to live on the farm."

"Teach her to live again in the wild," Trey answered.

"How?" his father pressed. "You saw for yourself yesterday that she has no fear of strangers. It is illegal to hunt does, I know, but she'd fall victim to the first man with a rifle that she walks up to."

"She lived in the wild for almost a year before we took her in. She'll remember some, and I'll teach her what I can, and she can learn the rest from all the other deer she meets in the woods. She'll be all right. And Tawny will be free." Trey was determined to carry out his plans.

Part III

_9_

HIS WAS THE LAST STOP on the school-bus route. The big yellow "troop carrier," as his father called it, lumbered up the long gravel road toward the farm. The bus was empty except for Trey and the driver, and the boy sat, as always, in the very front, right behind the driver's seat. He stared over the man's shoulder, through the windshield, at the road winding ahead through the forest. All the windows were open to catch a cooling breeze, and road dust settled upon the vacant seats. Trey enjoyed this part of the trip without the other noisy kids.

"This always used to be my favorite day of the year," said the driver, Frankie Mansfield, the fire warden's son.

"Mine, too," Trey answered, although he could think of a few other days in the year that ranked just as high.

The bus rolled to a stop at the fork in the road at the top of the rise. Trey hopped out, carrying his green book bag weighted down with a school year's worth of clutter and keepsakes. "I'll see you in September, Frankie," the boy called.

The friendly driver waved good-by. "Have a good vacation, Trey. Don't do anything I wouldn't do, and if you do, don't get caught!"

With a hearty laugh, Frankie ground the gears into first and the bus rattled away. The boy headed up the quarter-mile-long road to his house. Trey heard the distant sounds of his father's working tractor. Spreading manure, Trey thought. He smelled the rich, sweet odor in the air.

On both sides of the road, broad corn fields sprawled over ten acres. The young stalks stood ankle-high in long parallel rows. By August, Trey would be able to lose himself among the towering, golden-tasseled cornstalks, but that was a long time away, he thought. A smile came to his face when he considered the many leisure weeks that lay ahead. Summer vacation!

Tawny met him at the end of the circular driveway. She fluttered her tail and trotted beside him. She, too, seemed to know that today was a special day.

"Well, Mr. Mantle, were you safe or out at third?" asked his mother in greeting. She stuck her finger into the new hole in his trouser leg and tickled his knee.

"Safe!" Trey announced proudly. "We beat Mr. Lehey's homeroom ten-to-eight at recess."

"I'll have to remember to patch those before they

go into the wash," his mother said. The boy dug through his cluttered book bag and produced his final report card. His mother slid it from its cardboard envelope and scanned his yearly averages. Trey knew she would be pleased. He was a conscientious student who worked hard for his grades. Unlike his brother, Trey cared about how well he did in his studies. It was funny, Trey thought; even though Troy never seemed to do his homework, the twins invariably brought home identical report cards. Except for their "conduct" grades, that is: Trey's was always one letter higher than his brother's.

"Your father should see this as soon as he comes in," his mother said with a smile. "He'll be very happy." Math was Trey's worst subject and he had managed to get a B-plus for the last quarter: up a whole grade and a half from his mid-term score.

The steady, baritone-bass croaking of a big bullfrog set the rhythm for a chorus of smaller, peeping leopard frogs. The rich *ronk-ronk* belonged to an old friend; Ben-Him, Trey had named him. He sported a white dot of a scar between his shoulders where a B-B had glanced off his massive body. Luckily, the frog lived to tell the story of two trespassing teenagers who spent an hour "plinking" the life out of many unsuspecting frogs that sunned themselves in the grass.

Ronk-ronk, Ben-Him called into the night, simultaneously warning other males to stay away from his territory and inviting the smaller females into his lair. He ruled his muddy kingdom, now infested with clouds of black, squirming tadpoles, with absolute authority. Once, Trey happened to witness the foot-long amphibian swallow whole a smaller, spotted leopard frog. It had ventured too close to the bullfrog's realm.

Whip-o-will . . . whip-o-will. A whiskered whippoorwill joined the melodic night symphony from its hidden nest among the poplars.

Trey listened to the night's sounds and stared at his ready back pack on the floor beside his bed. Tomorrow, he and Tawny would venture alone into the forest for two days and one night: her first class in wilderness survival and the first time in Trey's life that he'd explore the forest without his brother at his side. He was a little worried about going it alone. Troy always used to make things so much easier.

Many summers before, Trey and his brother built a fort in the pines far from the house. It was a simple lean-to beneath a rugged granite cliff, covered with pine boughs and floored by the natural, thick coating of pine needles. The "courtyard," as Troy had called it, was carpeted by a lush covering of fragrant moss.

Trey surprised himself by finding his way to the fort so easily. It was the first time he had been there in over a year. The harsh winters had taken their toll. The shelter had collapsed under the snow; a mere skeleton remained. Trey began the long process of cleaning up and repairing the lean-to. Tawny busied herself, in the meantime, by tasting the scrawny blueberry bushes nearby.

The boy carted away the bare, gray pine branches that once formed the roof of the shelter. He found a faded and soggy pack of cigarettes amid the rubble and laughed in remembrance. Joel Ducharme, Troy's friend, had an aunt who owned the local variety store. Once a week, right before the school bus arrived to take them away, Joel and Troy used to sneak away from the school yard to the cluttered store where they bought a pack of cigarettes from Joel's older cousin. They would scurry back in time to catch the bus to the brothers' home, never mentioning, even to Trey, what they had done. And after a brief hello to Troy's parents, Troy and Joel would climb into the forest to the fort where they would spend the late afternoon secretly and safely puffing on whatever brand of cigarettes they had managed to buy for their twenty-five cents. Trey followed them once and caught the boys in the act. He threatened to tell on them if he were not allowed to join in the day's activities. Troy lit Trey's first —and last—cigarette with a wooden match.

The smoke entered Trey's mouth and he held it there, afraid to inhale it into his lungs, afraid to cough it out. It tasted rancid and hot, stale and sticky. Troy and Joel watched him closely; they smiled at each other. Trey held the smoke for as long as he could, then blew it out. The smoke hurt his eyes and made his mouth feel dry and burned.

"That's horrible!" Trey yelled and stamped the cigarette into the ground. Troy and Joel laughed at him.

"You have to get used to it," Joel said.

"Not me!" Trey promised out loud to himself. And, now guilty of the same offense, he swore never to divulge their shared secret.

Joel had locked himself in his bedroom and wept the night Troy died. Joel's older sister, Lynnie, had told Trey so, and he guarded that secret, too. Somehow, he felt closer to Joel now, even though he had been Troy's best friend and not his. Someday, Trey told himself, he would find a way to tell Joel how he felt. He tossed the crumbling cigarette package into a pile of sticks and brittle branches. Tawny sniffed at it and shuddered. Nothing good to eat there.

Trey worked quickly: cutting thick-needled boughs with his small hatchet and fitting them in place on the remaining support structure. He cut foot-long pieces of twine and carefully tied them securely to the cross beams. He added two walls to the lean-to, leaving the front open. He sat inside and watched the doe lying peacefully in the thick moss.

Lunchtime had come and gone before Trey finished his work. Quickly, he unloaded food and supplies from his back pack and unrolled his sleeping bag. Keeping one sandwich and a candy bar out, Trey buried the rest of his foil-wrapped food under a pile of moist pine needles to keep it cool. It would be a warm night, he thought, and decided to leave his bulky sweater in the pack. He rolled them both up into a pillow and left them at the head of his sleeping bag, right at the base of the shelter's granite back wall. He rubbed his hands with rotting pine needles to take away the stickiness of pine pitch from the freshly cut branches. Dark stains covered the palms of his hands, but he did not mind. No one would be telling him to wash up before dinner tonight.

Tawny grew restless. Unwrapping the chocolate bar, Trey broke it in half and offered a piece to the doe. "You'd better enjoy it while it lasts," he warned. "That's the last food I'm going to give you. You're on your own out here from now on." Tawny chewed the candy with a contented nodding motion. The wind hissed through the tree tops high overhead. A single shaft of light filtered down from above and warmed the boy and the doe in the courtyard.

After lunch, while Tawny napped in the sun, Trey climbed a towering pine tree and surveyed the country-side beneath. Through the trees, he saw the pastures of the farm and the roof of his house nearly half a mile away. His father drove the tractor over the field toward home. A late lunch today, Trey thought. The tractor looked like a toy from where Trey sat, high above the ground. So did his father.

In the opposite direction, Trey saw the cabin of the lookout tower above the tree tops. Mr. Durkey panned over the town with his binoculars. Trey wondered if the watchman had seen him. And high overhead, a solitary hawk swooped and circled. "When I die, I want to come back as a hawk," Troy declared one night as the boys lay in their bunks. Trey did not believe in reincarnation and he told his brother so. But now, Trey wanted very much to believe in his brother's ability to return. He watched the great bird closely as it hung in the air and played with the wind with its wing tips. He soared with the bird and imagined himself looking down over the countryside. He floated effortlessly, weightlessly through the sky. Suddenly, the hawk tucked its wings to its sides and plummeted downward with unbelievable speed. It streaked through the tree tops and disappeared. Another late lunch, Trey thought.

Tawny did not like the idea of Trey's sitting so far above the ground and she told him so with a snort of disgust when the boy climbed down to her side. "You're worse than Ma," Trey said. The doe accepted a good scratching between her ears as Trey's apology for having frightened her with his acrobatics.

They moved through the forest together. Sometimes, Trey stripped the leaves from an appetizing bush and offered them to her. He worried that Tawny was not eating enough on her own. The farm life was too easy for her, he thought; she'd become lazy and it was his fault.

Trey discovered three baby porcupines clinging to a low-hanging branch. They were harmless now, he knew; their quills had not yet formed and the young animals sported a soft black coat. But he did not touch them; the scent of humans would disturb the mother. The trusting babies huddled close together and looked down at the boy and his doe, curious and calm. But their mother was not pleased by the intrusion. Suddenly, she waddled out from the underbrush, her barbed quills bristling, and swung her heavy tail side to side. Trey barely had enough time to step out of the way before she turned and attacked from the rear. "She's not fooling around, let's get out of here!" shouted the boy. They scrambled through the trees and watched from a safe distance. Trey recalled those nightmarish times when his own dog, Jippy, staggered home with a mouthful of hideous porcupine quills. It took many hours and a good pair of pliers to pull them out.

The mother porcupine climbed up the tree and joined her young. Slowly, they shinnied farther up the tree to their nest where they were safe and cozy. "Remember this lesson, Tawny," Trey instructed. "Never play around with another animal's little ones. They don't like it at all." Tawny sniffed the air and headed northward.

She led the boy to a stream where the water splashed and gurgled over granite boulders. She drank from a tiny pool and Trey washed his hands and splashed his face with cool water. He sat on a moss-covered rock and pulled off his sneakers. The water felt wonderful on his feet. Tawny nibbled tender young ferns nearby.

This was the high ground where Tawny would spend her winters. By late autumn, herds of bucks and does would move into the area and stake out their territories. Tawny would be one of them, Trey thought, and was glad for the chance to see her winter home before deep snow closed it off.

The forest grew darker as the sun sank in the west and Trey moved back toward camp while there was light enough to find the way. Tawny followed obediently. Their fort was no secret to the other animals in the woods. Neither was the place where Trey had hidden his food. Squirrels and chipmunks scurried out of sight as they came into view. Trey saw torn bits of aluminum foil littering the ground. One bold red squirrel tugged at a remaining sandwich and a fat raccoon sat among the piled pine branches, sputtering and nibbling on a candy bar. The raccoon did not abandon its post, even when Trey approached within touching distance. It chattered loudly and went back to its snack. "Well," Trey said to it, "at least you're friendly." He recovered what was left of his dinner and placed it under his sleeping bag.

Tawny sauntered toward the raccoon and reached for its candy bar. At first, the animal was confused and stubbornly held onto its prize. But Tawny persisted and the raccoon dropped the candy from its tiny, humanlike hands and scurried away. Tawny finished off the treat. "Thanks a lot, girl," said Trey. "You just ate my breakfast."

Trey snuggled down into his sleeping bag as soon as he had finished his meager supper. Tawny settled on the soft moss and fell asleep. There were no dangers in the forest, Trey told himself. He and the doe had relearned that fact in one day.

The ghostly hoot of an owl drifted through the trees and the night air filled with the songs of crickets and whippoorwills.

"Well, girl, are you about ready to do some more exploring?" Trey asked. Tawny was restless to begin the day and had nuzzled him awake an hour before. He picked up his canteen and headed up the shadowy rise, around the sheer face of the granite cliff. "Come on," he called behind him, and Tawny followed. He marked the trunks of the massive trees as they ventured farther into the forest. He did not want to lose his way back to camp.

They walked quietly through the woods for an hour. Occasionally, a chattering chipmunk darted across their path, its tail held high in alarm. They moved through the underbrush in the opposite direction from where they had been the day before. Trey had never explored this stretch of land. He wondered if anyone had ever seen what he saw at that very moment.

Tawny found it first: an old, rutted, overgrown logging road that wound lazily through the trees. Years and years ago, the farmers in the area used to band together in the summer once their planting chores were over and select the best trees for lumbering, using great crosscut saws, double-edged axes and heavy wooden, ox-drawn sleds. It was no easy feat cutting, pruning and transporting fifty-foot-long tree trunks out of the woods to the local sawmill. The operation was a full-season one which paid the men handsomely for their efforts. The extra cash helped to make ends meet during the long and fruitless winter months. Trey imagined himself a burly lumberjack as he and the doe followed the trail. Tawny helped herself to mouthfuls of tender green leaves and trotted on ahead.

"Hey, look at that!" Trey called to her and pointed up the road. On the right, at the base of a steep hill, stood a gigantic loading platform. It was constructed, log-cabin style, like a huge wedge. The lumbermen used it as a loading dock, rolling the heavy logs down the hill, onto the ramp and then upon a waiting ox sled. It stood twice his height and Trey decided to scale it.

But the great logs were very old and rotten. They crumbled under his weight as he climbed. Tawny stood at the base and thumped her front hoof in warning. Trey sat upon the uppermost log and dangled his feet in the air. The logs groaned and shifted suddenly.

Before he knew what had happened, Trey found himself pitched forward amid the sounds of splintering and rumbling logs. The loading ramp had collapsed! He hit the ground and felt the air squeezed from his body. Slowly, the sounds faded away and the massive logs settled among themselves.

Tawny appeared out of the underbrush and licked his face. He lay on his back with a log across his chest, trapped. It hurt to breathe or even to move slightly. He tasted blood. Judging from the pain in his legs, he knew that a second log lay across his knees, although he could not look up to see for sure. Frantically, the boy tried to wriggle free. He dug his hands into the soft earth and tried to push himself out from under the crushing weight. Nothing. He pushed at the log on his chest; it would not budge. Tawny stood protectively over him.

"Home, Tawny," Trey gasped. His feet turned colder. The blood had stopped flowing below his knees.

Tawny did not move.

"Go *home*, Tawny!" he shouted with all his strength. A sharp pain pierced his chest. "Get Pa. *Go home!*"

The doe turned and started down the logging road, but stopped a few yards away and returned. "Go get help," Trey said. Tawny licked his face.

"Get out of here!" Trey screamed, and frightened the doe. She bolted through the woods.

Did she understand? he wondered. He had frightened her. Maybe she ran away into the forest. Maybe she wouldn't get help at all. He did not know. He could only wait.

He might have slept for a while, but he did not remember doing so. Now the forest was dark and cold. Again he tried to free himself, but his legs were heavy and lifeless and his arms too weak to move the log on his chest. A light rain began to fall and it cooled his face. A mosquito buzzed in his ear. The boy's head felt light and dizzy; he took short, painful breaths. And the numbing cold crept slowly up his legs.

It was quiet alone there in the forest. Deathly quiet. Where were they? Trey hummed a song to fill the silence and to drive away his fear.

Another hour passed.

"Trey? . . . Trey?" His father's voice floated through the trees.

"Here, Pa!" the boy yelled, but the wind was against him. He knew he could not be heard.

"Trey?" The voice grew louder, then faded away.

"I'm over here, Pa. Tawny?" he hollered. He heard the faint, tinny sound of her bell.

"Tawny, bring Pa this way." Trey looked through the forest for the searchlight. "Pa, I'm over here!"

"I hear you, son. Keep talking, I'll find you," his father answered at last. The boy's voice guided his father toward him. Trey saw a flashlight approaching up the logging road. Tawny ran ahead and licked the boy's face. "You did it, girl! You found Pa!"

His father knelt beside him and quickly examined his son's head and arms. "Can you move your legs?" he asked his son.

"No, sir. They feel cold."

"How about your chest?" His voice was calm and soothing.

"It hurts when I breathe. A sharp pain."

"In one spot?"

"Yes, sir, on my right side."

"Cracked a rib, I bet." His father panned over the ground with his light. "Now, where's your hatchet?"

"Over there. I stuck it in that old stump."

"I'll have you out of there in two shakes of a lamb's tail soon as I find a good lever." He moved away and searched for a young tree. Trey heard quick chopping sounds off to his right.

"This should do it. Try to wiggle your toes." Trey could move them only slightly. His father wedged the pole under the log and leaned into it. The log squeaked against the others and rose off his legs just enough for his father to move them out from under the weight. Trey's legs burned and tingled. He felt sparks in his feet.

"Try to move them now," his father instructed. Trey found that he could move his legs, with great effort.

"Good," his father said. "I don't think anything's broken." He moved toward the other log.

"Now, when I lift this one, you're going to have to slide out on your own. Okay?"

"Okay."

"You sure you can do it?"

Trey planted his heels and dug his hands into the soil. "Yes, sir."

109

"All right, then. When I count three. . . . Ready? One . . . two . . . *three!*" He strained and leaned upon the lever. The log rolled slightly and rose up. Trey felt a fleeting, stabbing pain and slowly wriggled out from underneath.

"Okay, Pa! I'm out." The log thumped to the ground as the others shifted and settled.

"I don't think I can walk just yet," Trey said, almost apologetically.

"You just rest easy and let me have a look at you," his father returned. "A couple of gashes and bruises. A good cut on your lip and probably a cracked rib or two. I think you'll live." He relaxed and settled down on the ground beside his son.

"I followed the hash marks on the trees," he said at last. Trey moved his legs a little more easily.

"I didn't want to get lost," said the boy. His father chuckled.

"No, I bet you didn't!"

"Good old Tawny," said Trey. He reached up and scratched the doe's stomach. She appeared quite proud of herself.

"She came to the back door while your mother was fixing supper. At first, she thought that Tawny'd just sneaked back for her usual hand-out, but she raised such a ruckus in the back yard that Ma fetched me from the barn. Tawny led and I followed, and here we are. Took forever to find you, though."

"Yeah, I know." They laughed in relief.

"I think I can walk now, Pa," Trey said at last.

"Okay, we'll take it slow and easy. I'd offer to carry you except you've gotten so big Tawny'd have to get a whole rescue party to tote me back after my heart attack."

Slowly, they walked through the forest. Trey leaned on his father for support. Tawny led the way.

"How did that happen, anyway?" his father asked.

"You don't want to know," Trey answered, glad to leave the incident behind.

_10_

BY THE LATE AFTERNOON, huge, black, flat-bottomed thunderheads collected over the town. It was an unusually hot day, Trey thought. The heavy humidity stuck to his body and soaked his shirt. And there was no trace of a breeze; the sticky air remained perfectly still, weighing down on everything beneath. Smoke rose from the kitchen chimney in a straight column. The menacing clouds blackened the sky and rumbled, grumbled and groaned as, called into battle, they continued to jam closer together.

The Landrys had plenty of warning. "This storm's going to be a doozie," his father said. He fastened the shutters closed with pieces of wire. Trey removed the light aluminum furniture from the back lawn. There would be no fireworks this Fourth of July, he thought. Mother Nature would provide the excitement.

"I sure hope the roof holds up," his father said. "I should have known better and repaired those shingles long before now." Trey peered deep into the clouds.

"It's a good thing we delivered the milk this morning, though," he continued. "If the power goes off, at least we won't have to worry about its turning sour." He closed the last pair of shutters and tested their hinges carefully.

Except for distant thunder there was not a sound in the air, not an animal or a bird in sight. They, too, knew what was about to happen and had taken refuge in their forest homes. Tawny scurried about the yard. Where would she hide?

"She should go back to the barn before the sky opens up," his father said. Trey led the skittish doe back to the safety of her pen.

Before he left the barn Trey knew the storm had started. The roof echoed the static sounds of hail-stones and rain pelting the building from all sides. The wind was not far behind. The boy ran toward the house through the storm. Hailstones, the size of marbles, beat down on his head and shoulders. They bounced and rolled over the ground and pinged against the hood of the tractor. As he reached the front lawn, a tremendous gust of wind lifted the boy off his feet and deposited him upon the ice-covered grass. He scooped up a handful of hailstones and ran to the door.

"Look at these!" Trey yelled to his parents once he was safely inside the kitchen. The spheres of ice clattered across the tabletop. His parents stared through the picture window and watched the storm rake the forest. The tall pines swayed violently in the wind.

Suddenly, the tallest tree at the edge of the forest began to fall, slowly at first, then it dashed itself against the ground. It tore a great hole in the earth and its exposed roots reached ten feet into the air. A fallen giant, toppled by the invisible wind.

Rain poured from the sky in torrents. Water covered the kitchen window in cloudy sheets, obscuring the view completely. His father studied the ceiling.

"Break out the pots and pans," he said calmly. Water soaked through the plaster and dripped to the floor in the corner of the room.

Great gusts of wind heaved back and forth, clattering the shutters against the house. Trey ran into the living room, carrying a stew pot to catch the leaks. Sooty rain water streamed down the chimney and soaked the ashes in the fireplace. With the windows closed off to the outside, the room felt eerily calm.

Pat-pat-pat. A steady dripping from the ceiling spattered the rug by the hearth. *Ping-ping-ping.* The first drops hit the bottom of the empty receptacle.

Snap! A shutter ripped from its fastenings and blew away. Its mate beat against the house, threatening to smash through the glass. Then it, too, disappeared with the wind.

CRASH! Lightning struck nearby and bleached the air with its vivid white light. Trey ran back to the kitchen. It was the loudest sound he had ever heard.

"The lookout tower was just hit," his mother said. Her voice sounded weak and thin.

114

"Do you think Mr. Durkey's all right?" asked the boy.

"Sure," his father reassured. "Just like the barn and the house, the tower's equipped with lightning rods. But I'll bet the explosion scared him both ways to Sunday!"

"It sure scared me!" Trey admitted.

"How's the living room?" his mother asked.

CRASH! Another lightning bolt struck just over the hill.

"The shutters were torn off," Trey yelled over the thunder. He tried to appear calm.

The big pane of glass in the kitchen window heaved and bowed with the wind. Trey worried that it might break.

"I think I'll call Frank just to make sure he's really okay," said his father. He picked up the phone in the entryway. It was dead.

"Well, that takes care of that!" he said.

The lights flickered and died.

"And that takes care of *that!*" his mother added. Trey fished through the cupboards for candles.

They moved into the living room and lit three candles. These glowed merrily and filled the room with a peaceful light. Trey and his mother sat close together on the couch. The black clouds opened again and flooded the helpless countryside. The skyline flickered and shuddered with lightning and thunder.

Trey stared at the mammoth red maple tree in the

front yard. Its great trunk creaked and leaned with the wind, its leaves shredded by the gales.

Lightning flooded the sky for an instant.

"Tawny!" Trey screamed.

"What?" his parents yelled.

"She's outside, under the maple tree!" He ran to the front door. It flew open and yanked free of his grip. The springy crab apple tree whipped back and forth. Trey ran into the rain.

"Tawny!" he called. She huddled close to the base of the tree.

"Trey, get back in here!" his father called.

"No!" Trey answered.

"Get out from under that tree!" his father commanded. Trey struggled to move the doe. She struggled to remain. Rain poured over them, making it impossible to see. The wind pushed against his body.

"Here, leave her to me. Get back in the house," his father ordered. He scooped up the doe and carried her into the house.

Tawny lay peacefully on the wet braided rug.

"She wanted to be close to us," Trey said. His mother rumpled his hair with a towel as he pulled off his soggy clothing.

"Instinct is taking over," his father returned. "You forget, the rest of the deer in this world have to weather storms outdoors, finding shelter where they can."

Trey watched through the front window as a huge limb, torn from the maple tree, thudded to the ground exactly where he and Tawny had been only a few minutes before. Wind whistled and howled through the house. Lightning opened great, jagged veins across the sky.

And then the storm stopped. As if some giant hand had closed a valve in the clouds, the rain stopped and the winds died down. Only the sounds of running water remained. Trey stood at the front door and searched the night. Far off, beyond the hill to the south, he saw the rolling clouds flash-lit by distant lightning. The air felt cool and clean. The storm was over.

"Let's not have another one like that ever again," Trey said. He led the doe back to her pen to spend the rest of the night.

When he returned to the house, the candles flickered and sputtered in puddles of milky white wax. It's time for bed, he thought, and wondered when the lights would shine again.

"It's a good old-fashioned milking day," his father said in greeting. "The phone's working, but we won't have electricity until later on in the day."

It was a bright, calm morning. Trey hopped over puddles as he and his father made their way to the barn.

He used an old face cloth and a small pail of soapy warm water to wash the cow's udder. She chewed on her breakfast of hay and grain. Tawny watched the boy closely. Trey slid the short, three-legged stool closer

117

to the cow and placed a galvanized bucket under the cow's milk-swollen bag. Tenderly, he grasped the first of its four teats in his hand, squeezing and pulling downward at the same time. He allowed the first spray of milk to hit the floor to prevent any impurities from contaminating the rest of the milk.

Sssssssst. A thin, steady stream of milk squirted into the pail. Alice, the elusive barn cat, circled the boy and meowed.

"Here you go," said Trey. He directed the stream of milk toward her. The cat stood on her hind legs and caught the milk in her mouth. It poured down her belly. She purred loudly. This is going to take forever, Trey thought. He and his father worked through the morning before they finished milking the fifty cows by hand.

Silently, Trey and his father walked over the corn fields, surveying the damage from the storm the night before. The long, fragile leaves on the knee-high stalks were shredded by the wind; they flapped in the breeze. In some areas of the field, in the lower spots, whole stands of corn were leveled and the plants lay on their sides in deep puddles. Trey cut ditches in the mud with his hoe to let the water run off so the plants would not drown.

"I told you that storm would be a doozie," his father said. He did not sound surprised or disappointed. Trey felt angry and helpless. It would be weeks before the fields were healed, he thought. If they ever recovered from the disaster.

"How can you be so calm?" Trey asked.

"Wouldn't do any good at all to get upset. There's nothing a man can do about the weather except let old Mother Nature run her course," his father answered and returned to his work.

It isn't fair, Trey thought. All his life his father had worked these fields and it seemed to him that the going got tougher every year. People complain about the price of milk, he thought, but no one really understands what it takes out of a farmer to supply it. He and Troy used to talk about the day that they would take over the family farm. They shared great plans for the future. Trey wondered if he could ever work the farm on his own. It just seemed impossible.

It was sundown before they finished their work. Trey's arms and shoulders ached and throbbed.

"Why don't you go upstairs and soak in a nice hot tub," his father suggested.

"Yeah," Trey returned, exhausted. He pulled off his mud-caked boots and walked through the kitchen.

As he lounged in the steaming water, Trey felt his muscles relax. He imagined knots of tissue loosening. Slowly, the pain melted away. He heard the steady rasping of a crosscut saw coming from the front lawn. His father had begun dissecting the huge fallen limb. The boy rested his head back on the edge of the bathtub and placed a moist washcloth over his face. It hissed, inflated and deflated as he breathed. He did not want to think about any more work until morning. He had time for a quick nap before dinner.

The rain-swollen pond was murky and cold. Water gushed from the culvert and poured through the fields. Trey burst through the back door and bounded merrily down the hill. Tawny followed the boy and leaped into the air. "It's better not to feel the water first," he shouted over his shoulder and plunged into the pond without breaking stride. Down, down he swam, following the weedy bottom. The water got colder and colder.

He surfaced thirty feet from shore, where Tawny stood. She thumped the ground with her hoof, summoning the boy back to dry land. "Come on in, Tawny," the boy called. "It's nice!" Gingerly, Tawny placed her foot into the water and backed away quickly. Trey laughed at the doe and floated on his back, squirting a stream of water high into the air through the space between his front teeth. With a quick kick, he turned and swam toward the middle of the pond.

Panicked, Tawny tried to follow, but only ventured belly-deep at the water's edge. Slowly, she circled the pond, lifting her legs high as she sloshed along. She nibbled on water plants and jerked away whenever a frog jumped across her path. Trey swam to the far side of the pond and made sure his feet did not touch the muddy bottom until it was absolutely necessary. He sat on the bank and waited for Tawny to join him. A tiny leech stuck to his arm and Trey watched it for a moment as it slowly expanded and shrunk back into itself. He brushed it away. Slowly, Tawny approached, still chest-deep in the water.

"See, it's not all that bad, is it?" Trey asked the doe. He ran his hands over her legs and scraped the water off. Tawny shuddered and headed up into the woods.

Trey climbed upon the huge fallen pine tree and walked along its now-horizontal trunk to where a great ball of roots and earth towered over him. A deep scar had been torn into the ground when the tree fell. The hole was filled with rain water. Already, little leopard frogs had made it their home.

Chuck-chuck-chuck, a plump woodchuck chattered at the other end of the toppled tree. Huge pine boughs now covered the entrance to her burrow and she did not seem pleased. She sat upright in the sun and watched the boy carefully. Trey knew not to approach too closely. A mother woodchuck, guarding a nestful of little ones, could cause some pretty serious damage to an intruder's arms and legs. Those long yellow chisel-like buckteeth were not for show.

"Chuck-chuck yourself," Trey said to the shiny-coated rodent and followed Tawny into the pine grove.

A crow cawed and flapped overhead, trying to escape the hecklings of two angry blackbirds. A comic scene, Trey thought; the big bird appeared so frightened of the smaller ones that fluttered above it and pecked at its back. "Why don't you pick on somebody your own size!" Trey called after the blackbirds. A square-winged deerfly bit his arm. "You, too," Trey said to the insect and swatted it before it could fly away. A yellow welt rose from the skin.

Hidden among the shadows of the forest, delicate lady's-slippers stood, seemingly untouched by the storm. Tawny sniffed at their pink, bulbous blossoms. "Remember this, girl: never eat a lady's-slipper," Trey told her. The wild orchids were very rare, an endangered species. They had to be protected at all costs. Tawny decided instead to nibble on a cluster of mushrooms nearby. Trey hurried to inspect them to make sure they were not poisonous toadstools. He saw tiny holes in the caps where insects had burrowed into them. They were safe, he told himself. "Never eat a mushroom that bugs leave alone," his father had told him. A gray squirrel climbed headfirst down a tree with one of the mushrooms in its mouth. It seemed upset that Tawny had discovered its personal harvest.

Tawny followed a pair of bluejays out of the woods and across the field. They screeched loudly. The boy followed the stream to a tiny natural bridge of rock and sat over the water, watching Tawny drink. She waded downstream. Adi left the herd of cows on the hill and joined the boy and his doe. She had grown quickly over the last couple of months; she stood much taller than Tawny and weighed three times as much as the deer. They romped like children over the pasture. Trey stayed behind on his bridge and studied the water.

Actually, it was Troy's bridge. He had discovered it first and, whenever he wanted to be alone, Troy would wander downstream and sit upon the granite shelf and just stare into the water for hours at a time. It was funny how his brother needed to be by himself sometimes, Trey thought. Maybe, every once in a while it was a good thing, he decided. Once Tawny was gone, though, Trey would be alone all the time, whether he wanted to or not.

Slowly, Tawny was weaned away from her diet of hay, grain and ensilage. She had to learn to find food on her own, Trey and his father decided. So every morning, right after he had helped with the milking, Trey led Tawny into the underbrush surrounding the farm and together they browsed among the bushes and young trees. The boy stripped oak leaves from their branches and fed them to the deer. He watched as she casually nibbled tender shoots and buds. Unlike domesticated animals that eat mostly when they are fed once or twice a day, deer in the wild eat little bits at a time, all day long.

Clover was her favorite food and Tawny enjoyed exclusive grazing rights to the hill behind the farmhouse where even the cows were prevented from going. Trey loved to sit in the sun and watch Tawny stroll over the field and taste the sweet-blossomed clover. It seemed that every day he uncovered another four-leafed clover. He had quite a collection pressed in the fifth volume of his encyclopedia.

His mother told him that she thought he was worrying too much about Tawny's eating and ignoring his own meals.

His father complained that he was spending too much time away from his chores.

_11_

THE ROLLING, ten-acre field was covered with thick, waist-high alfalfa that moved with the wind in flowing waves and shimmered in the hot August sun. It was time for the season's second haying.

Trey rode with his father on the back of the tractor; he studied the fearsome, saw-toothed cutting blade coupled to the tractor's hitch. It was raised straight up into the air and rattled and swayed back and forth as the tractor moved ahead.

They rolled past the front lawn, and Tawny trotted behind, but she stopped at the edge of the driveway and stayed close to home. She knew there was work to be done and did not want to get in the way.

"See you at lunchtime," Trey called to her. The doe turned and strolled toward the back of the house.

"Here's where you get off, son," his father said. He put the tractor in neutral and adjusted the hand throttle so that the machine idled quietly. "I don't want you falling off the back and into the cutting bar.

It'd turn you into mincemeat in no time." Trey stepped away as his father lowered the six-foot-long blade. It rattled when it hit the ground.

"Careful now," his father warned before he engaged the driving mechanism. The blade shuddered and jumped to life, its bottom set of cutting teeth moved quickly side to side.

Trey leaned on his long wooden hay rake and watched his father shift gears again and open up the engine. The tractor pulled away; the cutting blade sliced a wide path through the grass. His father circled the field twice, laying the grass down in his wake. The air filled with rich green smells. Once he opened a wide enough turning space at the edges of the field, his father would begin his back and forth mowing from the middle, working outward in both directions.

"It's going to be a hot one," Trey told himself. The sun glared down from a cloudless sky. He peeled off his long-sleeved shirt and tied it around his waist. Dust and itchy hay seeds stuck to his sweaty back and chest. His mother approached, carrying another long-handled hay rake. Their work was about to begin.

Pheasants flew like bullets through the air from their hiding places in the tall grass.

"Careful you don't get a sunburn," his mother warned.

"I'll be careful," Trey promised.

Trey started first, extending his rake to arm's length, letting it fall and pulling the mowed hay into long, straight windrows. His mother began a second row as soon as he was a few feet ahead of her.

"I thought Pa said last year that we'd have a power rake by now," Trey complained. This was the type of work he disliked the most. Raking hay was tedious and tiring. Most of the other farmers in the area owned a special piece of machinery that, when towed behind a tractor over newly cut hay, collected the grass into perfect windrows with long wire tines. Last autumn, Troy cut out an advertisement from an issue of *Farm Journal* and showed it to their father over dinner. Like most farm machinery, a power rake was expensive, but the boys had been assured that the next year they would never again have to spend hot summer days wielding hand rakes.

"Your father figures it just isn't in our budget to buy one this year. It was a hard winter, you know that, and we're still trying to scrape together enough to buy our own baler." His mother tied up her long hair in a red bandanna. Trey knew that purchasing a baler was a major investment. Every year that he could remember, his father "rented" a baler from one of the larger farms in town. The fee was one bale of hay for every ten produced: a costly price, especially since their own herd of cows was growing larger every year. Their own farm could use that extra hay, that was for sure.

"Be patient, Trey," his mother continued. "We'll have all the equipment we need in the next couple of

127

years." But in the meantime, Trey thought, the family would have to work half again as hard to make up for the loss of his brother. He just could not see how he could ever run the farm on his own once his father retired.

It seemed like weeks had passed before the family decided to break for lunch.

"Where's Tawny?" Trey asked when they reached the front lawn.

"I don't know. She was here when I left," his mother said. "Why don't you take a quick look around while I get lunch ready?" she suggested. Already, Trey had begun to cross to the back of the house.

"Tawny!" he called, but she did not appear.

He circled the pond, checked around and inside the barn, even scanned the pasture where the herd of cows grazed and lay in the sun. She was nowhere to be found.

"I can't find her," Trey said. He flopped himself down on a chair at the head of the table.

"She'll turn up," his father said calmly. He did not share his son's concern.

"I'm sure she's just off exploring on her own. A girl's got to keep herself occupied, even when the man in her life is off at work," his mother said. She placed a tall glass of iced tea beside his plate.

"Maybe she ran away," Trey said, almost to himself. He did not feel very hungry or thirsty. Nor did he feel like going back to work, although he knew he must.

128

Just as Trey had expected, the afternoon dragged by and he became more impatient for the work to end as each minute passed. Finally, he heard his father say, "Well, it's about time to call it a day, don't you think?" Even though his whole body ached and felt drained of its strength, Trey ran back to the house where he hoped Tawny would be waiting.

Still she had not returned.

"How about a quick dip before supper?" his father asked. The hair on his arms was caked with dirt and hay seeds. His face was streaked with dark lines of dust.

"I guess so," Trey answered. He worried that Tawny would not return.

They walked slowly down the hill to the pond, leaving pieces of clothing in a trail behind. The water felt wonderful, Trey had to admit. He felt magically rejuvenated, cool and clean.

His mother tossed towels to Trey and his father as they walked into the kitchen. "You look like new men," she said.

"I think I'll have another look around and see if I can find Tawny," Trey said.

"Don't be long about it. Dinner will be ready shortly," his mother returned.

Trey pulled on a short-sleeved shirt and, for the first time all day, he realized that he had not been as careful as he had promised his mother. His shoulders were bright red and felt hot to the touch. He tugged on a pair of shorts and left the house by the front door. Tawny was nowhere in sight.

"What could have happened to her?" Trey asked at dinner.

"She's not lost, that's for sure," his father said. "Thanks to you, Tawny knows every square inch of the entire hill. She's okay, I'm sure of that."

"But will she come back?" Trey persisted.

"It's not like Tawny to leave without saying goodby," his mother said. "Your father's right, Tawny's fine. Now, stop picking at your food and eat your supper."

He heard the faint tinkling of a bell and ran to the window. Tawny pranced up the hill, just in time for her usual mealtime handout.

"She's back!" he yelled and bolted out the back door to greet her.

"You scared me half to death!" he scolded the doe. "Where have you been?" Tawny nuzzled his chest, asking forgiveness.

"We told you she was all right," his mother said. Gently, she stroked the animal's glossy coat. "Welcome home, oh Prodigal Doe."

Trey ate his supper ravenously. He could not imagine how he could be so hungry.

"Kay-boss, kay-boss," his father called in a high, singsongy voice. He and Trey walked toward the barn. Tawny trotted behind and the boy made sure that he kept her in his sight.

"Kay-boss, kay-boss." Slowly, the cows moved toward the barn in a long single file. It was milking time.

Once the hay was sufficiently dried by the sun, Trey helped his father attach the huge, borrowed baler to the back of the tractor. It was like a great, rolling factory which Trey felt he could never hope to understand. As the tractor moved over the long windrows with the baler in tow, the hay was scooped up, compressed into heavy bales and bound tightly with two strips of baling twine that ran lengthwise around each bale of hay. As a bale reached the end of the machine's long shoot, it was pushed out onto the ground by the one behind it.

His mother drove the long flat-bed truck into the field, parked it and began working with her son to load the scratchy, cumbersome bales onto the back of the truck.

"How does that machine tie those little knots in the twine?" Trey had asked his brother once. "Elves," Troy had answered matter-of-factly. "They work for a nickel an hour and all the hay they can eat."

Tawny scampered around the truck, inviting the boy and his mother to join in her game.

It was difficult at first, but once Trey set his mind to it, he found that he could lift the heavy bales by himself. Last year, he had had to ask his brother for help in lifting the bales up to the truck bed.

A whole day was devoted to collecting the tons of

hay bales from the field, but their work was not yet over. One at a time, the bales rode the clanging conveyer belt up into the hayloft where, once again, they were hefted and stacked up to the rafters.

"Lifting hay bales builds strong bodies twelve ways," his father joked. Trey could count more than one dozen ways. Every single muscle in his body ached and throbbed.

"According to the *Encyclopaedia Britannica,* white-tailed deer are supposed to be excellent swimmers," Trey said to the doe. "I think it's about time you learned, don't you?" He led Tawny to the edge of the pond. They waded knee-deep into the water. Tawny tugged against her collar, refusing to go any farther.

"Don't you chicken out on me, girl," Trey said. He pulled on her collar with both hands, but Tawny resisted with stiff legs and a quick backtracking. "Whoops!" His hands slipped and Trey fell backward into the water with a tremendous splash. As if forgetting her own safety, Tawny plunged in after him. From beneath the water, Trey saw the doe swimming over the pond in a large circle. He pushed off the muddy bottom and surfaced beside her. "I knew you could do it!" he congratulated her. Nostrils flared, Tawny continued paddling around and around. She moved strongly through the water. "You're a natural," Trey coaxed. Soon, the doe lost her fear of the water and actually seemed to be enjoying herself. She swam alone to the far bank of the pond and waded ashore. She shook herself like a dog, turned and waded back into the water. Trey waited for her to swim to his side, and applauded her progress.

"We'll have you ready for the summer Olympics in no time," he called. Tawny looked pleased with herself and nuzzled the boy gently. "Don't mention it," Trey said. Now he felt confident that Tawny could make it on her own out in the wild. Yet he dreaded the thought of having to set her free. There's plenty of time for that later, he told himself.

Toward the end of August, it was time again to venture out into the lush fields. This time, Trey helped to attach the threatening forager to the back of the tractor. It towered over the boy and his father, its long, curved shoot arched ten feet into the air. Great, pointed wedges extended out front like fangs. The tall rows of corn were combed and collected by the menacing, protruding half-cones. The juicy stalks were then pulled inside the huge machine and, with a great whir of chopping blades, mulched and sprayed out the shoot and into the back of a high-sided truck. His mother and father worked closely together: he driving the tractor and guiding the ensilage machine, she handling the truck and making sure she did not drive too close or too far away from the spout so that the silage would miss the truck and be sprayed to the ground.

It was feed corn, specially bred to grow fast, tall

and thick. "Not fit for human consumption," Trey declared. The yellow ears grew so large that Trey could not wrap his fingers around them. The fat kernels were dry and pulpy; they tasted starchy, like paste. Not at all like the juicy-sweet butter-and-sugar corn that they harvested for themselves earlier in the summer.

Trey rode in the truck with his mother. Tawny, upon hearing the clattering racket of the forager, had decided to remain in the barn where it was cool, dark and quiet.

Each truckload of ensilage was transported back to the barn where a noisy, vacuum cleaner-like machine sucked up the sweet-smelling mulch and spewed it into the two tall aluminum silos for storage until the barren winter months.

Trey always felt sorry for the corn fields after they had been ravaged by the harvest. They looked scarred and barren as they lay dormant, waiting until the next year when planting season would start the cycle all over again.

Tomorrow, clover and winter rye would be planted over the bare fields to replenish the soil and to prevent erosion by the harsh wind, rain and snow.

Pheasants have nowhere to hide any more, Trey thought.

After supper, Trey led Tawny to the south pasture where she would join the cows and graze through the balmy late-August night until milking time in the morning. To the west, a great orange ball of fire settled into a brilliant pink horizon and to his left, in the east, a silver full moon rose slowly over the land. They walked peacefully together, stirring up blinking fireflies in their wake. I'm running out of time, Trey thought. Tawny will have to leave soon.

Adi stood beside the barbed-wire fence and scratched her chin against the top of a post. She mooed once. Trey opened the wooden gate and watched as Tawny and the heifer moved into the shadows.

"Trey, it's time to help with the dishes," he heard his mother call.

_12_

IT WAS a cool and calm September morning. Wisps of mist hugged close to the ground and floated over the newly-shorn corn fields. It felt like autumn, Trey thought. Already, the leaves of the maples and oaks showed signs of turning from their somber green to vivid reds and oranges. In about one month, the farmers in the valley would have to worry about the killing morning frost. Winter would come early this year, he decided.

Tawny appeared excited and restless by the hints of colder times to come. She loped across the field and kicked high into the air. A fat ring-necked pheasant fluttered from the underbrush and glided to safety at the far edge of the field. It scurried into a stand of tall sumac that glowed a brilliant red in the morning light.

Trey stood beside the barbed-wire fence and watched the doe scamper merrily around and around. School starts in two days, he told himself. Enjoy these free moments while they last.

And then Tawny saw them. Way in the distance,

moving cautiously through the mist, a stately buck and two does moved over the pasture toward the fruit-laden orchard on the other side of the farm. They had begun their migration into higher ground before hunting season and winter threatened them.

Tawny froze. She stood in the middle of the open field and watched them for a long time. Then, as if hypnotized, she walked toward the unnoticing deer. Slowly she moved, staring straight ahead.

"Tawny, no!" Trey yelled. He ran to her side, wrapped his arms around her neck and clutched at her collar. He dragged her back over the front lawn and led the doe into the barn. He saw his mother watching him from the living-room window.

She did not mention the incident to Trey when he returned to the house. They did not talk until after supper was long over and his father had headed off to bed.

"You couldn't let her go, could you?" his mother asked understandingly. Trey glanced up from his magazine and looked into her face. He wished that she had not witnessed his actions. He felt ashamed.

"No, ma'am," he answered and looked to the floor. "I love Tawny." He needed the doe. He feared being left alone.

"We all love her, Trey. She brought us something special when she arrived." And she would take that special something away with her when she left, the boy thought.

"I couldn't let her go. Not today. I'm not ready."

"But Tawny is ready, isn't she?" his mother asked.

"Yes."

"Do you feel sorry that you spent your summer teaching her to live in the wild?"

"Not really," Trey answered, but he knew he was lying. He regretted the day he first committed himself to setting Tawny free. "I just hoped that, maybe, she could live here with us and go to the woods whenever she wanted to," he admitted.

"Maybe she can. But we have to give Tawny the chance, don't we?" She was pushing him, Trey thought. But it wasn't that easy. Once Tawny left the farm, he might never see her again. Maybe she would forget him. He could not bear that.

"You don't understand," said Trey after a long pause. His mother crossed the living room and sat beside him on the couch.

"Oh, yes I do," she said in her you're-feeling-sorry-for-yourself-again voice. "Since the day you and Troy were born I've been preparing myself for the time when you grow old enough to live a life of your own."

"But I'm going to stay here and work the farm with Pa," Trey said.

"How do you know that? What if you go away to school and decide that you want to become a doctor or a businessman? Children grow up and leave home every day." But people have families, Trey thought. They visit each other and write letters and call on the phone at Christmastime.

"Your father and I have been preparing you—just as you have been preparing Tawny—for the day you leave your home. It's the same thing, you know," his mother continued. "And when that day comes, I'll set you free and tell you that I will always be here if you should ever need me. But I'll know that you are ready to face the world on your own."

"And when I set Tawny free, I'll know that she can make it on her own, too." I guess they are the same things, Trey thought. His fear of setting Tawny free was not a fear that she wouldn't survive. Rather, he feared that he could not go on by himself. Yet his mother had confidence in him. She believed that he would succeed.

"When someone truly loves another, he can't feel possessive, because that is a one-sided love that hurts the other."

"I'll never hurt you, Ma," Trey promised.

"I know you won't, Trey. But what about Tawny?"

He would set her free. Next week, as soon as school started.

He lay on his bed and stared out the window. His mother's words played over and over again. He felt ashamed of what he had done to Tawny that day. What would Troy have said to him, he wondered. If Tawny had been his brother's doe, what would Troy have done? He would have turned her over to Mr. French's Animal Farm as soon as she became a nuisance, that's what Troy would have done, he told himself. But he was different from Troy, just as Tawny was different from all those other deer at the Wild Animal Farm. He understood that now and he understood that this problem was his and nobody else's. Since the day Tawny arrived at the farm, Trey had done everything he could to make her happy and healthy. Everything, that is, except to give her the freedom she needed. He would prove that he could solve this problem on his own. The courage to be himself had to come from him and not from Troy or Tawny or from his mother and father.

He remembered another September day, many years ago, when Troy stayed at home with Joel Ducharme and left Trey to share the day just with his father.

It was a moment long forgotten until now.

He was five, and struggling through a late afternoon in the middle of September. The excitement of a bustling Haymarket Square had become stale and Trey grew cranky as his father continued to browse among the displays of antique jewelry, tools and furniture, fresh fruits and vegetables.

At first, it had been fun: the color, the people, the thrill of reaching between the slats of a snow-fence pen and sinking his fingers deep into the soft, musty coat of an unsuspecting sheep, one of many gathered noisily together.

Ducks in little swimming pools ate soggy bits of

bread. Nervous chickens exploded into frantic motion whenever he stamped his feet, leaving behind them a few tiny feathers somersaulting through the vacant air. They made him laugh.

But now, he was tired. It was late and hot, and even the comic white geese clustered nearby made sounds that scraped against him, like coarse wool on bare skin.

It was time to go home. Why didn't his father know? Trey wondered.

He pouted and sulked, yet they remained. Even tugging on his father's pant leg did not seem to help.

Two bumpy cobblestone streets came together into one, like a **Y**. And in the point where they met, a little fat man in faded overalls stood among the colored shadows under a cloud of balloons. Their strings tangled in his hand and he sang—almost to himself, although anyone could have heard him who had wanted to.

"Bah-*loons* . . . Bah-loo-oons," he sang. And then, a pause. The airy song floated over the heads of the unnoticing people.

"Bah-*loons* . . . Bah-loo-oons."

Trey turned as his father came closer, knelt on one knee and looked into his son's sullen face.

"You wait here a minute, okay?" he asked with his hand on Trey's head.

He crossed the street, his hands in his pockets, walking slowly. Trey counted his father's steps to him-

141

self. One . . . two . . . three . . . At eleven, he stopped beside the funny fat man. They nodded: once, twice. And his father gave the man some money from his wallet. Then the "Bah-loon Man" gave him every one of his balloons. Hundreds of them. Millions!

His father turned and walked back toward his son. People looked and pointed at the colors bobbing overhead. Suddenly, it was not hot any more, and Trey really loved his father. My father! he thought.

Trey ran to him, his hands reaching upward. He laughed and glowed inside. His father handed him the string of one green balloon. Trey wanted to hold them all, and he reached for his father's other hand. The man stepped away and Trey followed.

And when he got near again—just as he got within reach—his father raised his hand high over his head . . . and released them! All of them! My father, Trey thought. My father!

Now it was very hot, and Trey was *very* tired. He felt hollow and sick. In anguish, he gnarled his fingers into his father's trouser leg and exploded into tears. I hate you, I hate you, Trey screamed inside.

His father's hands fit neatly under his son's arms and he lifted the boy off the hard sidewalk. Up. Trey's arms wrapped tightly around his father's neck as he sobbed into his collar. Why?

"Look up," said the man with a gentle smile. And Trey did, through blurring tears, runny nose and all.

The balloons rose slowly, silently together, blown

side to side by the wind. Up, up. And as they rose above the buildings, crosswinds scattered them in all directions.

Scattered them, sprayed them through the sky. Gone.

Trey released the string he had held so tightly.

The one, lonely balloon rose straight above: green, slowly wagging its tail back and forth, back and forth. It rose until it was only a colorless speck in the autumn clouds.

A soft breeze cooled his face.

"You set them all free, didn't you, Pa?"

"Yes, we did. How about we go home now?"

Trey awoke at dawn the next morning. He studied himself in the mirror as he dressed.

"Trey, how do you and your brother manage to tell each other apart?" his kindergarten teacher had asked him many years before. He remembered that it was his first day of school and that he had wanted to make a good impression on his new teacher, so he thought for a long time before he answered.

"Well, ma'am," he said, finally, "when I wake up in the morning and look in the mirror, I know it's me!" The other children in his class had laughed at his answer. Even Troy, who sat beside him in the next row. He had thought he had given a very honest answer. He was confused. But not this morning. Trey knew now how honestly he had spoken that day many years before. It was his face he saw in the mirror. His and nobody else's.

Someday, when he became a father, he would name his first son Troy. He and his son would work the farm. He and his son would succeed, he knew that now.

Trey tiptoed through the house so as not to wake his parents. In the kitchen, he selected two doughnuts: one for himself and one for Tawny. He eased out the back door and made sure it did not slam behind him. Trey sang to himself as he ran. He would tell Tawny of his plans to set her free next week. He would be ready then. Today was the last day of summer vacation; he would make sure it was the most special day of all.

But his heart sank when he reached the barn and saw that the sliding doors were parted slightly. Slowly, he squeezed through the opening and walked into the barn. Tawny was gone.

"Tawny," he called, but he knew she was nowhere even close to him. He sat on a bale of hay and stared at the floor. Now, he thought, Tawny would never know that he, too, had wanted her to be free. She had run away from him. She feared him.

When his parents wandered downstairs and into the kitchen, they found Trey sitting at the table.

"She's gone," he said. "She got out last night and didn't even say good-by." His head felt heavy; he stared down at the empty table. "She's gone for good." Trey ran from the room.

That night Trey's dreams were filled with nightmarish images of Tawny lying helplessly in the woods, wounded and starving to death. Before he could make himself wake up, Tawny changed into Troy and then back into Tawny again. Maybe he hadn't taught her everything she needed to know, he thought. Maybe she needed him right now. He fell back into a restless sleep.

The new school year started the next day, Wednesday. Ordinarily, the first day of school was an exciting and happy day for Trey: feeling older and wiser than the kids in the lower grades, collecting his shiny new textbooks and moving into his own homeroom desk. Not this time. The day dragged on and on and, at recess, Trey found a corner of the dusty playground where he could be alone, away from Bruce Manson's stories of his visit to California and Linda Edwards's bragging that she had flown all the way to France on her summer vacation and that she could speak French even better than grouchy old Mr. Carpenter, the language teacher. Trey wanted to be alone, and he waited for three o'clock to take its own sweet time in getting there so he could go home, back to his room.

"How was your first day?" his mother asked, trying to cheer him up. "I made a lemon meringue pie for dessert. I thought we'd celebrate your becoming a big eighth-grader. How about that?"

"Fine," said Trey, answering both questions at once. He shut himself in his room and stared at the pages of his history book without reading the words.

The same nightmare appeared to him every evening for ten days. Finally, the dream stopped.

A light rain fell as they drove up the hill toward home. The leaves on the trees were brilliant reds and oranges. They had reached their peak by this, the third week of October.

Trey sat in the back seat, silently watching the windshield wipers beat back and forth. It had been a long sermon, he thought. Too long. He pulled off his necktie and stuffed it into his coat pocket. He wanted to change out of his Sunday suit as soon as he got home. They pulled into the driveway and parked the station wagon under the maple tree. Trey stared at the house.

"Trey, look who's here," his father said and Trey looked out the car window on the other side. Out across the pasture, he saw Tawny walking slowly toward them in the rain.

Trey threw open the door and scrambled over the stone wall. With arms outstretched, the boy ran and met the doe in the middle of the field. He hugged her tightly and kissed her nose. "You're home. I missed you," he said softly.

Tawny nuzzled his hand and stretched out her neck for Trey to scratch. She closed her eyes and looked very happy. The boy wrapped his fingers around her collar and started to lead the doe back to where his parents stood under the tree.

146

"Looks like Tawny brought along some company," his father said with a grin. He pointed behind the boy.

With a great snort, a buck sauntered boldly toward them. Trey and Tawny turned to face him. He stopped a safe distance away and reared his proud head. He thumped the ground again and again, summoning the doe to his side.

Trey released his grip on the collar and Tawny moved toward the towering buck. "Tawny!" Trey called. She stopped and turned to him. He ran to her and hugged her again. She licked his face and rubbed her head against his chest. He placed his hand around her collar and fumbled to release its silver buckle.

"You be a good girl, Tawny. I love you." And then, after a long pause, Trey said, "Good-by."

Slowly, Tawny moved away. She stopped and looked back at the boy. "Go on," he coaxed. The buck pawed the ground impatiently. She did not look back again.

The two deer touched noses once and the big male circled her slowly. Then, with a flick of his tail, they loped over the field to the far side to the pasture.

Trey waved his hand high over his head. "I'll miss you!" he called. They disappeared into the woods.

His parents stood on the lawn and waited for him to join them. Trey was glad that it was raining so they would not know that he was crying.

"Maybe she'll come back someday," Trey said.

"Maybe she will," his mother said, embracing him. "I'm awfully proud of you, Trey."

They walked to the front door where Trey paused

and studied the open field before he entered the house.

It's time to start again, he told himself.

Tomorrow, after school, he would bring flowers to his brother's grave.

It was their birthday.

ABOUT THE AUTHOR

Chas Carner was born on Long Island and spent his childhood in southern New Hampshire, the setting for this book. He graduated from Dartmouth College in 1974, having studied creative and screenplay writing, and now works as a free-lance writer for various media. *Tawny* is his first book.

Mr. Carner lives in New York City with his wife, Jennifer Kemeny.

ABOUT THE ILLUSTRATOR

Donald Carrick is the illustrator of many books for children, including *The Dirt Road, The Pond, Swamp Spring* and *The Brook,* all written by his wife, Carol Carrick; *Peter and Mr. Brandon* by Eleanor Schick; and *Christmas Tree Farm* by David Budbill. He and his family live in Martha's Vineyard during the winter and spend summers in Vermont.

ABOUT THE BOOK

The text of this book is set in Primer, a modern typeface designed by Rudolph Ruzicka. Display is in Caslon 540 Roman and Italic types, variants of those cut by William Caslon of London in the 1700's based on Dutch models of the previous century.

Type composition is by Fuller Typesetting of Lancaster, Pa.; the book has been printed and bound by Halliday Lithograph Corporation.

Typographic design is by Ben Birnbaum.